The Last of the First

By Mario G. Fumarola
Illustrated by Charles Favreault

Printed in the United States of America

ISBN Paperback 978-0-692-01402-5
ISBN Hard Cover 978-0-692-01402-8

The Last of the First

This book is dedicated to the millions of immigrants that passed though Garden Castle and Ellis Island to come to America from 1890 through 1939 most of them believed they took as much as they gave and still a few others knew they gave more than they took.

Contents

Preface

In two previous books, Mario Fumarola dramatized the two sides of the chiaroscuro of Italian-American life, the bright light of the immigrant *famiglia*, and the darkness in the harsh struggle of the immigrants to make it in America. Here, in the final volume of the trilogy, we have the children and grandchildren of the original immigrants (the "last of the first") facing the disappearance of the immigrant generations, for some few, the quick, ultimate sacrifice of death for the adopted country in war, for the others, the slow obliteration of the Old Country heritage in the assimilation into American life of people like "Tony," our representative of the three generations of Italian-Americans, from his joy at the street festival at the age of four to the suburban melancholy of this man who drinks too much in his seventies. But the indomitable will to live, and to live well, is still there in Tony, as he meditates continuously on his life and his death and their meaning. The book ends with counterpointing of the young Joey's death in war against the both sad and joyful fragments of memory and meditation of Tony's old age as he sits looking out on his beloved backyard: a poignant finale to a long poem of various tone.

Eugene Paul Nassar
Prof. Emeritus of English
Utica College
Founder: The Ethnic Heritage Studies Center

CALL
DAILY
3 teens charged in
Mexican beating death

BOYS
UTICA
PUBLIC SCHOOLS

From the Mountains…to the Prairies

We'll Call Him Tony

Pg Dn

We'll call him Tony, that's not his real name but, it fits the character and the story. Tony is an old man now, and his wife (and it seems all agree) thinks he drinks too much, but he doesn't think so. Even so, the 'kids' (those over forty) cut him a little bit of extra slack. It is like they have this (*I respect you old man…but you ain't always right*…attitude!) But he doesn't mind it, *What the heck!!! They are probably half right anyway.* He knows all that, and even knows he should not have that half of a stogie (or more) in the afternoon or evening.

But *what the hell you gotta live till you die right? Right???*

When Tony got up this morning he…*how do the artsy fartsy people say it?,* he did his toilet and then he went downstairs. Tony was never a breakfast eater, and in the old days, it was a cup of coffee, the newspaper, and an un-filtered Camel cigarette…a whore's breakfast they used say…excluding the newspaper, of course.

The newspaper was on the kitchen table with a rubber band around it; his son must have picked it up off of the driveway when he came home from work. He's been working nights for a long time. Tony poured his coffee, took a sip…he never liked his coffee too hot and it wasn't, so he decided not to put an ice cube in it to cool it off. He'll just let time cool it; since his retirement, every day was Saturday.

He stood by the coffee pot and took the rubber band off of the newspaper. The headline and lead story was "3 teens charged in Mexican's beating death" just like that, and Tony wondered why the newspaper only capitalized the word Mexican and none of the others words.

Beating…humm…beating…humph…three on one…the Mex was older…25…the kids, teenagers…one played football...two Slavic surnames and one Welch...drinking involved...and you can bet your ass...testosterone...hum, beating...heavy shit...it is not like sticking...jabbing a guy with a knife...or pulling a trigger...bang...far away or close...but beating...fist and feet...elbows and knees...fist...tight fist...swinging...hitting near the mark, on the mark...heavy shit...a guy is dead...Naw!!! I'm not gunna read the article...not now...not now...maybe later...too early for that shit...later, later...poor bastard...25 years old...poor bastard teenagers...they gotta live with that the rest of their lives...beating...a beating...

Tony shook his head and was sad for all of them; he separated the newspaper sections, found his Sudoku and then went to look for a pen. When he returned to the kitchen table, he saw that he had left the front page lying face up on the table and just reached down and flipped it over. *Naw!!! I'm not gunna deal with or think about that now...later...I'll think about it later...*

It didn't work…his thoughts always drifted back to the incident…and he'd drive it away…and it crept back…*naw...I don't wanna read the article now...I'll do it later...yeah later...not now!!!*

He started his Sudoku. He reached over and picked up his coffee, took another sip, and spotted a number that fit in the upper right hand square. He continued working on the puzzle, but after a while…when the numbers were not coming as fast, he looked out the window and squinted. He shook his head quickly and went back to the grid. He decided he'd get back to the puzzle later, he flapped and folded and snapped and creased the newspaper and finally landed on the sports page.

For what little good it did, he looked at the headlines and tried to concentrate on some of the action photos; but gave up. He went to the front page and read the lead story: "3 teens charged in Mexican's beating death".

What is new under the sun? What has happened that has not happened before, under different circumstances, what can happen that will not again be repeated sometime? Tony remembered that big dance scene from 'West Side Story' on the tenement rooftop, Puerto Rican kids dancing and singing Bernstein's music, the lyrics…*everything great in Amerika*…and the response…*if you all white in Amerika*!!!

Nothing new under the sun that was based on Romeo and Juliet…*dat was in Italy…your beloved Italy…not Spanish Harlem…what da hell??? Are we animals??? Will we ever be civil??? Green cards…wet backs…passports…visa…sponsors…who didn't come from somewhere else one time or another???*

Then his thoughts drifted to something else <u>his people</u> Ma and Pa, Zia Grazia and Uncle Dan, always patient and quiet, his Uncle Joe, Zia Grazia la fur-nara, all of them Zia Minucci all of them, poor Enzo. He forced himself to look at the headline again…"3 teens charged in Mexican's beating death", just the word Mexican capitalized…*guess it had to be…Mexican is a proper noun, I suppose, but teens…beating and death are not.*

Pg Up

Pa has been gone for a couple of years now. Angelo was away at the seminary and Salvatore was married with four kids already.

"Whadda time-a you get home lassa night?" "It was late Ma ...Yeah I know...it was very late" ...a pause... "You are gunna go to Mass aren't you?" "Yeah I'll go Ma...what time is the last mass at St. Ant-knee?" "Ya knowa...ya knowa!!...itza eleven thirty, like she always wassa...e piccata (it's a sin/pity) ifa you miss again!!!"

He cleaned up, dressed and opened a can of beer, pinched a meatball from the bowl and sat at the kitchen table. It was becoming a Sunday morning ritual, a cold beer and a couple of meatballs. *Naw, Ma I ain't goin to Communion.* After brushing his teeth he liked the cold taste of beer and the, almost, too hot fried meatball. It worked out fine for him on Sunday mornings. He wasn't dating anyone in particular at the time and Saturday nights were always special, more so if you had a job and couple of extra bucks in your pocket. *What the hell did we do last night???* He was trying to remember since he got up but only came up with bits and pieces. *Oh Yeah...we went to the beach and then stopped at Roach and Quinns.*

"Youa gonna go to church, huh???" "Yeah I'm going Ma." "We'll eat about two o'clock Okay? Sal is comin over wid the kids later ain't he?"

He was pushing open the screen door when his mother said to him, "Antonio…sta attenda…(stay attentive) we don't wanna no trouble…she repeated …no trouble and then added wida da otter people…and again no trouble!!!" "Yeah!!! Yeah Ma, I know."

It surprised Tony too, but he did go to the last Sunday morning mass and even found an almost empty pew on the right side of the nave…*the bride's side*...the side his father preferred. Try as he might not to, he still did his usual day-dreaming and people watching during the Mass. *(Now children when you are at Mass don't be looking hither and yonder...Christ is on that sacred altar...it is disrespectful and it is a sin…*and the second and third grades from Brandegee School that attended religious instruction in the church basement on Tuesday afternoons would bob their heads in unison and in chorus chant…*Yes Sister Mary Ann!!!)*

The Gospel and the sermon were said by a visiting Jesuit priest. They often came to Tony's beloved Saint Anthony of Padua Church to give a week of Lenten services. Tony lazily took note of his different black robe with the white embroidered heart on his chest and under his left shoulder, and wondered if this guy…*is gunna be filled with fire and brimstone…*

In a light-hearted conversation about various orders of priests, Tony's brother Angelo once told him, "You don't find too many dumb Jessies…dare all smart or dey don't make it!!!"

Tony brought himself out of the usual sightseeing state and focused on the padre on the elevated pulpit with its hand carved wooden cupola. He read the gospel of the Prodigal Son and then gave a sermon on his interpretation (because there are as many interpretations as there are sets of ears) of the message in the text of the Gospel's "Word of God"!

It was the Jesuit who reminded the parishioners that this Gospel is about three men…two brothers…and their sins …and a once again happy father with love for all his children.

Over the many years that followed, Tony would often recall that Jessie's sober sermon and be reminded how much more he was like either of the sons than the forgiving and loving father. And his mother's words too, would often echo in the crevices of his brain: *Sta Attenda*! (Stay alert)…*we don't wanna no trouble.*

The Melchiorre House

Pg Up

It was always the Melchiorre house. Although the Melchiorres never owned, nor were they ever its sole occupants, it was still referred to as the Melchiorre house. Angelo and Maria pay rent to N. D. Peters & Sons Construction Company. There were twelve families living in that framed three-story building and Tony was sure that not even one non-Italian family ever...*ever*...lived in that house. He was now seventy years old and he could still rattle off the families that paid rent there through the years.

There were the Melchiorres (naturally) and the Lo Contos, the Coliccios (at one time Tony had a crush on Annie Click), Parteleos, the Leones, the Parrapellos (Rosie with pig tails up until the seventh grade), the Convertinos, the Barlettos, the Pintos, the Cerminaros, the Valenzanos and the Pannellas, all with kids, all eating and sleeping and housekeeping and working. That framed three story structure was painted gray and had a good sized front porch for each level and a smaller rear porch for each level also. The front, first floor porch had five wooden steps, it was their stoop and the kids liked it better than the others because it wasn't as cold as the concrete stoops. Directly behind the building was a long, long, narrow garbage shed with twelve three foot doors opening into a four by eight cubical. Some of the tenants put locks on the doors (*like somebody was gunna steal their garbage*) and they all made sure all of their household garbage and stove coal ashes were out for the Tuesday and Thursday night collections (ashes on Thursday only).

Nick Laino Trucking had the city contract and their work crews would hustle down the alleyway to empty each stall...but only if the doors were open. Sometimes the tenants would sprinkle the ashes on the shoveled sidewalks to prevent someone from slipping, all the tenants did it on the days it would sleet.

If the Melchiorre House was a "she" and if she would claim all the families…the men who worked digging ditches for road crews or working in a steaming dye room who left early and came home late and hungry; their women raising children saving a penny here and a penny there, sewing torn overalls and mending socks, and happy because this was so much better than the misery in the old country; the noisy little kids, the older kids who spoke perfect Italian to their parents and also spoke perfect English on the street and started to learn about sex, the life and hustle, that lived and died within her bowels and her soul. She, the Melchiorre House would tell you she sent thirteen of her boys to far away foreign lands to defend democracy. She sent thirteen of her beautiful flowers and the joy of her youth to defend her, and others, because…"my country tis of thee".

N.D. Peters owned a similar house on corner of Kossuth and Catherine and just four houses down (traveling west) they had their construction yard. The yard had concrete silos and neat, square, flat-top mountains of cement blocks and a New York Central Railroad single track railroad siding entering from Broad Street. There were two gates, front and back, but all traffic leaving the yard, used Catherine Street; coming home they used Broad Street.

Large cement trucks with huge rotating drums/barrels would rumble out of the yard onto Catherine every workday. Those going west passed the Melchiorre house and Brandegee School: those going east, to Kossuth, had to stop by Tony Marraffa's fish store. There was a yellow and black octagon stop sign, with twenty-eight circular glass reflectors so as to be seen at night when the beams of headlights fell upon them.

Sometimes in the summer, the fleet of mixers would be starting at seven a.m. and earlier, and you could easily hear them lumber out of the yard. You could see and watch as those huge cement mixers lurched when…and as...the drivers shifted gears and sometimes you'd see a thin water tail splash onto the pavement. The trucks would seem to groan wearily as they left the yards and the silos. The mixers, like the road gangs, went out of the yard to build America.

The Caress

Pg Up

Johnny was still comparatively young, not quite eighteen, but close. He had quit school at sixteen, when it became legally possible, and was working at Uncle Joe's bakery. The older Melchiorre boys, Danny and Cosmo had already been drafted. Aunt Grace was leery about hiring 'family' but the War forced her to make a lot of concessions and furthermore, it was only a nephew and he wasn't living under her roof.

As strange as it sounded, *Zia Grazia...la furnara*...never really trusted her husband's siblings or their kids...she never really let go or forgot *that* incident way back when. Although all of Uncle Joe's sisters and sister-in-law were faithful church goers and prayed the Rosary and did novenas, she knew...and believed with all her heart...that *A volpe cambia la pelle, ma non il vizio!!!* (A fox will change it fur, but not its habits!!!)

The bakery crew had started at midnight to mix and shape and bake the bread. Johnny was now working six and half days a week. He didn't make much money...not as much as the other *old* workers. His aunt rationalized, that since all employees were given free bread every day...and since her sister-in-law had all those kids...Johnny took more bread than the others (sometimes she had to give him three loaves a day)...he was being compensated in another way and what they gave him was more than enough!!! Or at least, so she thought.

Johnny didn't complain, although he knew what was going on, and he even felt a little sorry for Uncle Joe. Especially when, at a convenient and discreet opportunity, Uncle Joe would quietly slip Johnny two extra dollars on a Saturday afternoon. As he handed over the money he would place his index finger on his lips, signaling silence...no fanfare. Uncle Joe preferred to avoid open debate with Zia

Grazia, *la fur-nara*, about money manners. Young Johnny was a good kid, the family, everybody, liked him; he was quiet, obedient, good-looking and a hard worker. He was a dirty blond among so many brunette and black-haired relatives.

And, Johnny had dreams and wishes and feelings and desires and some modest ambitions, and his youth reassured him that everything was possible and just around the bend.

This past Sunday he went to the movies. The Family Theater, right there on Bleecker Street, not too far from Kossuth Avenue. That night he was thinking about what was becoming an increasing urge, or fantasy, with John. He was becoming caught up in the patriotic fever of the days. It was the spring of 1943 and the newsreels and papers and the six o'clock news, sponsored by Mobil and the Flying Red Horse, were all talking and showing and printing stories about brave young men fighting a war in far off lands like, Russia and the Philippines and Australia and Guadalcanal and Wake Island. *Guys just like me!!! Some of them even look younger!!!*

When he left the theater, he had thirty-five cents left in his pocket and he was hoping the guys he was with wouldn't suggest going to a coffee shop for a piece of pie and coffee. He wanted his money to last longer, and he thought, *Maybe, I should give Mom only one of those two dollars that Uncle Joe snuck me. I give her all of what Zia Grazia gives me. I wish Mom would give more me money to spend on myself.* But then, he felt a pang of guilt like he was being selfish. The guys were going to go to the coffee shop; Johnny begged off and made some lame excuse. He gave them a short wave as they walked away.

He waited a second before he crossed Bleecker Street, a trolley car was heading west, going downtown as it passed he noticed about five soldiers frolicking in the rear of the trolley car. At least two of them had an open bottle of whiskey in hand and all of them were singing at the top of their voices. John stopped in his tracks and just looked at them as they passed and then just stood there on the curb watching the trolley car disappear down the line. For some reason, and he wasn't sure why, he envied them.

That scene haunted him for the longest time. To him it was a sort of freedom, an adventure into excitement, to new places, strange languages…yes, a freedom and money in his pockets to buy cigarettes and a bottle of whiskey.

It was a Friday, and for a multitude of reasons, they ran much later than normal. But, finally, well after ten o'clock, Uncle Joe lifted his peel and placed it in the cradle along the far wall. Uncle Joe, not being that tall, had to raise his arms and the bread peel almost over his head, eye level at least, to reach the cradle. He was tired. He thought, *this batch will bake in less than three quarters of an hour and then I can go upstairs, get something to eat and get some much needed sleep.* He's been up since noon yesterday.

The three full-time bakers, the older ones, had already gone home and it was just young Johnny and him in the back while his wife was in the front room, by the large menacing black National Cash Register machine. She was filling orders for the nearby grocery stores and restaurants. There were eight such deliveries, four grocery stores, Tony Marraffa's Fish Market, and three restaurants all within the neighborhood and in easy walking distance. It was Angelo, Tony's second older brother who would make those deliveries, carrying the bread in a large basket.

During school days, Angelo would run straight from Brandegee School to the bakery on his lunch hour to make these deliveries. On real busy days, like a Friday, he would have to make several trips back to the bakery to complete the rounds with his basket. Johnny and Angelo's Uncle Mike had left more than an hour ago, making the long truck run to the Argento farms and the Deerfield bean picker's shacks at the Westerners' farms.

Young Johnny went to his last job of this or any workday, and began to scrape the encrusted bread dough from the odd shaped agitator in the mixing machine. It wasn't a pleasant job, long and tedious, and it seemed forever before you were able to coat the agitator blade with oil and be done. Even then, if you wanted, you could easily find a spot or two you missed, or discover you forgot to do the back side of a blade. At Uncle Joe's bakery they used to use what was called a RASPA, a baking tool with a metal plate/blade and a wooden handle firmly riveted into place by three brass rivets. It was designed to cut dough and occasionally would, of course, require re-sharpening.

Angelo, serious and industrious and intelligent, did not go to school this particular Friday. Jimmy, as Uncle Joe liked call to him, because the boy reminded him so much of his younger brother Enzo and because he had difficulties distinguishing between Vinny and Jimmy (one of the very few attempts Uncle Joe made to become Americanized) was sick with a sore throat. He had to have his tonsils out. His mother and father lamented the fact that they didn't take them (the tonsils) 'out' earlier, when he was four, or five, or six. Now, that he is almost twelve and the tonsil troubles became more frequent, it was becoming more painful and more uncomfortable and more expensive to correct.

Nonetheless, 'Jimmy' worked hard those six days a week at the bakery and on Saturday afternoons, after he's finishing sweeping the entire bakery, Uncle Joe would give him a roll of pennies, fifty-cents wrapped in a reddish maroon paper wrapper. Making sure his wife was out of earshot, he'd slip Jimmy a dime and with the same signal instructing silence (index finger to his lips) he'd muss his hair and tell him to be a good boy.

Angelo would run to the bakery as soon as he got out of school for lunch. He would make eight bread deliveries in less than forty minutes, using a wicker basket (like those still used for laundry today). When completed, he would run home and wolf down his lunch. Seldom was he ever late getting back to school by the one o'clock bell.

"Zia Grazia...Angelo didn't go to school today...his tonsils are hurting him", one of his many cousins reported. A dilemma for Zia Grazia...*Aglia!!!* Uncle Mike left long ago and would never be back in time for the deliveries. John...yes, John is still here. "Govanni!!! Govanni!!! Venga a qua!!!" (John ...John come here!!!)

"It won't take long," she told him, "less than half an hour. Maybe you can do it in two trips...make sure you count the breads you leave at each stop....count 'em twice...let me know if there are any returns...tell the owner how many you are leaving and how many you are bringing back. It is important because your uncle, or I, will go and settle accounts tomorrow afternoon...count the loaves twice...I'll count the loaves you bring back...understand? (Compecce?)"

"Yeah...sure Aunt Grace...sure!!!" was the good kid's reply to his stern aunt...who had no children of her own...but secretly so wanted them. What she had was a husband with certain long ago and foolish youthful indiscretions and lustful miscalculations. None of which she could ever truly forgive.

Johnny made two runs...he did the groceries stores, the fish market and Goomba Joe's restaurant (Dominic gave him a cold beer). Then, Tomaso's first and finally John Cappocio on Bleecker street and Kossuth Avenue.

Old man John Cappocio, was not there, he had taken his old car, a 1927 Studebaker, and gone to the farmer's market by Mt. Carmel Church. He went to get some greens and hot peppers and maybe a couple of bushels of good, ripe tomatoes. On the way back, he was going to stop by the slaughterhouse on Catherine Street, the one closer to Hubbel Street than Mohawk Street. Pino De Grace told him he would save all of the cows' stomachs (tripe) he got that week for him, and only him. Tripe was a big thing on Saturday afternoons in the old neighborhood.

Hard working men, with three or four dollars in their pockets…some with even five…would stop by, play some brisco and maybe have a couple of tournaments of 'boss'. They'd all snack on bowls of tripe in a very hot tomato sauce with some bread and cold beer. The men…because of their background and upbringing (many of them from the mountain sides of Abruzzi and le Puglia)…had no concern about etiquette or proper table manners and hungrily devoured many, many bowls of tripe with chunks of bread…ripped or pulled apart with strong, callused hands. They would mop up any sauce left in their bowls with the chunks of bread until the bowls looked freshly washed.

The system in the kitchen was that the cook would ladle the food (usually tripe on Saturday) and place the bowls on the worktable, near the door to the bar. John Cappocio, was the only one to portion the bread; a quarter of a loaf for two bowls and half a loaf for three or four orders. The whole loaf of bread, which was stored on a shelf above the worktable, was quartered or halved by a very large knife. The knife always remained upon the prep table in a certain spot, between two stacks of saucer plates.

The customers…most often the regulars…would critique the contents of their bowl… "It was hotter last week", "This is cooked perfect", "The tripe is soft", "The tripe is gummy", "Momma mia, this is hot…gimme a nutter beer", and some said nothing. And, those who said nothing were often the wisest.

Nobody, never…ever…commented on the quality of the bread. They were simple hard working men from the hills of Italy and from a poverty they just could not live with, and to most, bread was truly manna from the heavens.

The kids in the old neighborhood (Tony, Joey, Angelo, Salvatore, Donnetta, DeeBee, etc.) grew up with an expression…which was translated into English…and was to become a very true and sincere compliment when describing someone else. To call someone…*un pissa de pane…a piece of bread…*was to say many things about him or her: uncomplaining, quiet, obedient, respectful, trustworthy…all those good things. If you'd ask an old timer…the immigrants in the neighborhood…why they came to America…many would simply say, "Per lo pane…for bread." There was a very deep and almost reverent meaning to the word: Bread.

It was like saying: Life.

But the key to life for John Cappocio was the trick of the sauce…the sauce had to be…must be…for the survival of the business…extra spicy and extremely hot. How else was he ever going to sell six kegs of beer on a Saturday? He calculated he sold more beer on Saturday afternoon than any other time…Friday and Sunday evenings were a distant second.

The tripe and bread was only fifteen cents a bowl.

The story goes that Cappocio had a wife and three children in Italy. And, he had shot and killed a man in the village square after a heated and violent disagreement. Then, he ran home, took half the money his family had saved and fled to Naples. He told his wife that when he made a lot of money, he would send for her and the children. He booked passage to America and in spite of becoming involved on the fringes of the old bootleggers who went to Canada for pure alcohol…he did neither of the two – make lots of money, or send for the family.

With some minor connections, and well after Prohibition was repealed, he became partners in a bar and lived in the apartment upstairs. His partner died shortly thereafter and John Cappocio found himself the sole owner of a nice little bar on Bleecker Street and Kossuth Avenue. In time, he settled in and made a life of it. But, soon, it was getting harder to run the bar alone. On one of those rare trips to the Canadian border to pay respects to some friends out of the past, he met a fairly young girl through her father. They met in a bar and the girl's father, who spoke only French (she translated in her very heavy French accent), complained of the lack of work and any opportunity for him or his daughters.

So it came to pass, that this stoic girl, who whenever she spoke, spoke very softly and with a very thick French–Canadian accent, returned with Cappocio to be his cook at the bar and…share his bed.

Common Law marriage was very foreign to the culture in the neighborhood, just as it was in the old country.

The ladies in the neighborhood would refer to her as *La Francese*, the men, would half smirk, bob their head to the side and say…*John's Commara* or just *la Commara*…the girls would giggle and say she was half French and half Indian. "Look at her long black hair and those dark eyes…she only talks to men, if she ever talks," they would whisper. She was not very tall, petit (like the French say) and the young boys would fantasize at the shape of her calves, the slope of her shoulders, the bronze like color and clearness of her cheeks, the perfect shape and size of her breasts…like a Greek statue…a zillion times better! And, more often than not, they had to fight off 'those' sinful and lustful thoughts…

Bless me father for I have sinned...I have had impure thoughts and desires...

Yes my son, and how many times...have you ever spilled your seed...how many times? I firmly resolve, with the help of thy grace, my son, I absolve you of your past sins...now, go and sin no more!!!

When he arrived, *La Francese,* who was in the kitchen, unlocked the side door for Johnny, (they didn't open until twelve). If Cappocio wasn't there by noon, she would open all the doors, turn off any heat on the cooking range and step behind the bar.

"I got eight for you today…no he is sick…yes he'll be working tomorrow…where do you want me to put the loaves…up there? Sure, I can hand them to you if you want…you got two returns."

There was a table…a worktable…in the kitchen by the doorway into the bar area, it served as a prep table to fill orders from the bar and dining room. About three feet above it was a shelf, it was long but narrow, and was an ideal location to keep and store foods and supplies. The table's surface should always be as clear and clean as possible. *La Francese* wanted the bread on that shelf and arranged in a special way as to make it easier for them to retrieve the loaves, one at a time, as needed. Angelo knew the system and she would let him stand on a milking stool, hand him the loaves and have him stack accordingly.

Now, she pulled out the stool from under the table and volunteered herself to step up on it and stack the bread. Johnny reached out a hand to help support her and in acknowledging the gesture; she smiled and nodded her thanks.

Boy!!! She's got small feet, John noticed when she was finally up and ready.

He handed her the loaves one at a time, while standing on the stool, her chin was near the top of his head and her breasts…the shape and size, like a Greek statue, were at eye level for him…and it awed him. Like a robot, he kept handing her the bread and his eyes never moved from this most beautiful sight.

And then, as if his mind had no control of his actions, he reached up and placed his right palm on the breast nearest to him. He knew what he had done, but…he could not help it…he had to!!

La Francese stopped her routine of stacking the loaves on the shelf and looked down at him. She looked straight into his eyes with a surprised look on her face. The realization of his act finally hit John. He was ashamed…he was embarrassed…he looked away…he shook his head like he was trying to erase the memory…and he lowered his hand. He tried to talk but his mouth felt like it was filled with cotton, he shook his head again and tried to say he was sorry. But, no sound came out. His eyes showed the pain of his embarrassment and *La Francese* saw this from her perch. She placed a hand on his shoulder and stepped down off of the three-legged stool, never taking her eyes off his face. She stood quietly facing him and said nothing.

Bless me father for I have sinned...how many times...impure thoughts...impure desires...how many time...how many times...I don't know...I don't know!!!!!

Johnny finally forced himself to look at her face…it too was beautiful…and said, "I'm sorry, I am really sorry! I...I…I couldn't help myself…I'm so sorry…"

She looked back at him and into his sorrowful eyes, half smiled, reached down, took a hold of his right hand, twisted it slightly, raised it and placed it palm down upon her breast. John slowly spread his fingers and caressed it. To John, it was warm and firm and what he thought to be…gently soft…and he could not believe it was happening to him…*to him*!!!

She seldom, if ever, saw such honest innocence, such tender desire as she was seeing now. This boy…this man…young and strong…clean with smooth cheeks and neck, who smelled good…like bread and fresh air...was close enough to enable her to feel the heat from his breath and to hear his excitement in his rapid breathing.

With that same uncontrollable body reaction, Johnny bent over slightly and with the gentleness only a lover possesses, kissed her softly on her cheek. *La Francese* turned her head just a bit and seemed to be looking at the floor. Johnny kissed her ear.

La Francese faced him again, stood on her toes, and kissed him on his lips. She slowly lowered herself back down on her heels, paused, raised herself again, closed her eyes and kissed him again. Her tongue passed his lips and touched his. John embraced her.

She had gotten used to the smell of stale beer and cigar smoke and being muscled about in bed and elsewhere, and now…like it was a reward for all the hardships of the past…she welcomed and accepted his acts of gentleness and sincere caring.

And there…right there…three months before John went marching off to war…between the work table and the wash tubs…under a loaded bread shelf…*La Francese* and Johnny melted into the floor and made love. John lost his virginity and she…after so many years…finally felt an ecstasy she never experienced before and fulfilled a carnal instinct. From that day on, she knew and sincerely believed she was a woman, regardless of her dull and unappreciated existence.

La Francese…stoic…petit…fragile…very, very old before her time…died before young Johnny came marching home in the fall of 1945.

The Schoolyard

Pg Up

There was, of course, the boy's door and the girl's door at either end of the Brandegee School and because they, like all good children, were instructed to always obey the rules they used the segregated portals to education, thus remaining forever pure, innocent and un-violated. Well…up until they moved on anyway.

Kindergarteners and up to the third grade were allowed a fifteen minute recess in the morning and then again in the afternoon. *Dats the way it was all over da world!!!* The whole world had recess for fifteen minutes every morning and every afternoon. The kindergarten teachers would come out to watch and supervise their brood, like giant hens over noisy…happily playing little chicks. There were two first grade classes and two second and third grade classes. The teachers would alternate on a daily basis and go out into the schoolyard and stand vigilant at various posts. They were there to maintain order and watch for scraped knees, and to remind kids to use their handkerchiefs. The bell, way up there by the roofline, was partially enclosed under a small frame roof and reinforced wired glass door, but it was open on the sides.

At nine-thirty and at two-thirty and fifteen minutes thereafter, an electrical current would surge into it, activating the hammer to clang loudly against the circular brass of the bell. The housing for the outside bell was not put there to suppress any sound; it was put there to protect the mechanism. When the bell rang, you could easily hear it anywhere…anywhere on earth…down way past Kossuth Avenue and Marraffa's fish market, almost to the middle of the nine hundred block of Catherine Street. It had to be!!! It was designed to be heard over the shouts and yelling and of the young children at play.

First grade…recess…"Hey Tony did ja see doz pictures in da book when Mrs. Moonaratti was readin to us???" "Yeah sure…dey were great!!!" Maybe it was John and Jane…(See Jane Run) or some other, but it was about two children who went out with their parents to look for a new home. They made several stops and as Mrs. Moonaratti continued to read, the parents found some sort of fault with all but the last one.

"Whadda ya tink about all dose houses they turned down? My mudder and fadder would have bought anyone one of 'em if dey had the bucks!!!"…and Tony answered…"Mine too!!! Ya know da one I liked the very best???…Was dat yella one wid bedrooms upstairs and a big front door and a yard as big as half this playground and it was up on a hill and wid ah pointed roof and it even had a yella garage and dat had a pointed roof too!!! And lotsa room for a dog to run around…giant dogs like Marraffa's got or even Rin Tin Tin…I'd give a zillion bucks to live in a house like dat…two zillion!!!"

"I liked da one wit…" and they would each have their own little dream of something other than a rented four or five rooms and cold-water flats and alleyways and garbage sheds in the back yard. It was easy to do.

And Tony and one of his buddies who lived in a framed three-decker right next to the Melchiorre house, continued to dream on. Tony remembered feeling better off than his friend, because he lived in a three-story brownstone. It was made of solid red brick.

Kindergarten…recess…the schoolyard without grass…just cinders from the boiler room…"Hey Joey wasn't dat a good story 'bout dose tree pigs…da one dat built a straw house and the utter dat built a wood house and the smart one dat built it wid bricks! Boy dat was scary!!! My brudder Angelo told me da wolf got so tired tryin to blow down the brick house he fell down dead and the pig in the brick house cut his gut wide open and saved his brudders…dat makes me feel a lots better…didn't ya brudders ever tell ya dat???"

Tony wasn't really sure why he liked that story that Mrs. Moonaratti read to the class, but he did like it. In time and as he became older, he remembered…especially when he was in bed on those windy and cold January and February nights when he could hear whistling sounds and see the curtain move an inch or two…and you'd find that sweet warm spot on your half of the bed…and get warm and feel safe…the pull chain light is still on in the kitchen…Pa is reading the paper…Ma is darning socks…*I wish I didn't always make holes in the toes…must be the toenails…da big toenail…dats hard like a rock and pointy too!!!*

I'll huff and I'll puff and I'll blow your house down…but only the windows rattled and chattered…only the windows. *I am warm and I am safe and Ma and Pa are in the kitchen and Salvatore and Angelo are in bed wid me.*

Second Grade recess period…*Angie gave me six beauties (marbles)…I love da one that got blue in it and looks icy…gotta play good…don't wanna lose any of 'em to Johnny or Fast Vinnie…or Buster…Buster is a good player too…Johnny hunches…he is a big cheater…always calls for seconds when he misses da first time…and when he makes it on the second try he sez God proved it…he's a liar…maybe I'll dare Vinny to a game…he's not as good as dem utter guys…* "Hey Vinnie…Vinnie wanna play???" Tony hated to lose…he would never put his beautiful blue beauty in the game.

Angie, can I keep this blue one forever???

Pg Dn

This is a nice wine…must have been a good batch. *Ah what the Hell…ya know they shoot it up with chemicals anyway…but it's good.*

Tony lit up the stub of his one daily cigar. He had to twist his head way down towards his shoulder and push his chin forward, as far as possible, to avoid singeing his lips and nostrils. Looking down his nose he saw…maybe sensed would be more accurate…that the flame was close enough to the cigar tip and sucked in. The flame seemed to quickly point to the tip, it was a good contact. Through the bluish gray smoke, he sent a stream of breath at the match head and snapped his wrist to guarantee it was totally extinguished.

For no apparent reason, he looked off to the left of the screened-in patio and back toward the house. He noticed that his wife had already cranked in all of the weather proof, super-sealed windows on the first floor (he couldn't tell if she did the second floor windows) enclosing the screens and ergo winterizing the house. For a microsecond, Tony first wondered why, and then when, she had completed that chore.

He reminded himself…*Well ain't it dat time of da year???*

He remembered that after his father died….

Pg Up

…it was up to him to install and remove the six huge wooden frame storm windows in the flat. He remembered them as being huge, awkward and clumsy, and above all, heavy. He remembered too, you first had to get the storm window outside the brownstone's double hung windows. You had to open the bottom portion of the window, lift the storm window horizontal, snake it outside as far as you could reach, square it away, using only your wrists and arms (and half hanging out the window), then rest the storm window onto the concrete and very slender sill for a minute…Take a deep breath…*upsy daisy*…and at the proper angle fish around for the two hooks on the top sash…way-way abovc. It was done by sense…feel …judgment…guessing…because you could not see the outside hook/bracket. Pa would perform the task uncomplaining; his youngest son would do it in a cloud of blue angry smoke and a Niagara of profanity.

For a couple of years after Tony married, he would continue to do that dreaded 'duty' twice a year. And then, in time…the spring (la primavera)…when Tony would half-heartedly say, "Ma ya want me to take down the storm windows?"

"Naw…ancora e fredo…pui tardi…(no it is still cold...you can do it later)"

She, ironically, eased Tony's conscience and made him feel better by telling him she was getting older…she was always cold…the summers were getting shorter...it saves on the heat…and the small oval, two by eight air vent cut into the base of all of those bulky storm windows would let just enough fresh air into the house…when…and if needed. He never remembered the original vent flaps, what Tony remembered were those that Pa whittled out from the siding of wood wine crates. Sometimes a strong gust of wind would not only rattle and let all the glass panes chatter, those wooden vent flaps would do the same.

Pg Dn

Sometimes...with or without an alcoholic stimulus...Tony's thoughts drift to the curtains bellowing just a tad...the sound of the wind howling and rattling the glass…those big, old storm windows would sound like they were chattering in the cold...*I'll huff and I'll puff and I'll blow your house down...but I have found the sweet warm spot in the bed…I am warm…the 100 watt light bulb…with its ribbed...like a half moon...glass globe is on in the kitchen…I am safe…Ma is sewing socks and Pa is reading the paper.* Later on, after he winds the yellow clock with the cowboy and horse and lasso, Pa will pull the string and the light will go out and the kitchen will be dark.

But I am safe…warm…da blanket is all da way to da top of my ear…da wind's blowin…huff and puff…ya ain't gunna blow my house down…

SANTO'S TOURS

To the Oceans…White with Foam

The Telegram

A Ripple Effect

Console the Grieving

American Legion Visit

Looking For Something Better

The Telegram

Pg Up

His name was Mr. Nichols Louie. He was a nice guy. A long time ago, while in France, he made sergeant during the First World War. He was assigned to an engineer unit and when he first got there, he dug miles…and…miles of trenches. In time, he was reassigned to putting up communication poles and stringing wire, a forerunner of the Signal Corp. He often joked about always being a target, either way up in the front lines shoveling dirt, or a little bit to the rear climbing high poles. You dug and picked real fast to get below the Prussian's line of fire, but when you were up there on a pole stringing wire your only desire was to return to terra firma, not end up under it. It had taught him a very different and sinister definition of sniper.

He remembered a lot of things about those days, and in time, the sharp edge of fear dulled and the glossy red of blood on bandages faded. He remembered too…and never really forgot…the Red Cross gave away cigarettes on the front line. The Army would get Camels and the Navy service men would get Lucky Strikes. Nick never knew why, but they did. He has since given up smoking, but when he did, he smoked Luckies. Another thing, being of German heritage, he never liked it when the newspapers or politicians talked about the enemy…the Germans…he preferred Huns or Prussians, because he felt he was neither, his grandfather was Bavarian. And even now, after September first of 1939, he preferred they not call the enemy Germans…but Nazi.

When his grandfather came to America he settled in Wisconsin. His father found a job on the railroad and eventually worked for the New York Central Railroad. He met and married Nick's mom in Utica and they made it their home. When he was real young they lived on Bleecker

Street, eight hundred block and right across form Holy Trinity Episcopalian Church. Bleecker Street ran parallel to Jay, Catherine and Broad Streets.

Broad Street was really not any broader than the other streets, but it went all the way to Albany and Buffalo and was to become Route 5. There were, and still are, a string of brick factories and mills that line the north side of the street from Culver Avenue almost up to Union Station. Here and there a railroad siding line would snake and cross Broad Street, at construction yards. Those that serviced the factories and mills were contained between the factories and the streets. The New York Central operated at least eight lines directly behind the factories and those lines paralleled the Barge and Erie Canals.

After WWI, Nick found work, married and had three beautiful daughters (and he is the first to say they all resembled their mother). The eldest will be graduating from Utica Free Academy this June and has aspirations to become a nurse.

Mr. Nichols Louie works for the Western Union telegraph office on Genesee Street. He is the afternoon supervisor from 1300hrs till 2300hrs. The staff…the old and very young alike…even his peer supervisor…and the district manger, all call him Mr. Louie. The man's poise, experiences and demeanor automatically, and without asking for it, demanded that type of respect.

It is the late spring of 1945. A very depressing winter had just passed and Mr. Louie will never forget this past February, with its heavy casualty of the Battle of the Bulge and Iwo Jima. Now the heavy fighting on Okinawa was winding down, and the War Dept Notices appeared to be decreasing weekly. He thanked God. Strange sounding places he had never heard of before…Bastogne…Iwo Jima…Okinawa…he wasn't even sure if he was pronouncing the names properly. He often recalled years and years ago, in the fifth grade classroom, there was a large wall map made of a plastic cloth. It would be rolled down for the class to see and with a snap would roll up and disappear. As you looked at it…it would show the Northern and Southern Hemispheres in the center, Europe and Africa and Middle East on the right and Asia and the Pacific Ocean on the left. The teacher, with her long wooden pointer (it had a black rubber tip on it shaped like short bullet) would stand before it and she would enlighten her brood, "Japan is an island nation, what other Pacific nation is also an island nation?…Rebecca???...Good!!! The Philippines…and now who can tell me where Alsace-Lorraine is???"

Mr. Louie remembered there were barren white areas on the map, mostly around the Arctic and Antarctic and some small…kind of like bleach stains on a colorful print…white blotches in Africa and the Pacific Ocean. The teacher explained, "Those are unexplored regions, but this is an old map and many of those areas are being or have been explored. In a very short time…certainly within your lifetime…there will be no unexplored area on Earth."

In time, Mr. Louie learned that Iwo Jima, Okinawa, Leyte, Guadalcanal, Bastogne, Normandy, were all part of his new world. He thought too, *have these ... these Island Nations, uncharted and unexplored areas, become sacrificial altars for the young male lambs??* Because Mr. Louie was such a nice guy, thoughts like that depressed and saddened him greatly.

At times like these, Mr. Louie often recalled an old Italian he once met and chatted with at a wake. This old timer was a member of his father's section gang for the New York Central. It just so happened that one of their co-worker's…a burly Lebanese… youngest daughter (only six years old) died. Young Nichols was made to accompany his father to the viewing. "It is a matter of respect to a good man, a good worker my co-worker and his family…we must offer not only our condolences, we should see if we can help him and give a little something in an envelope…we can not do much, but we can do something!!!"

In those days, viewings and wakes were held in the deceased's house or flat and on very rare occasions in a church basement. When the coffin was displayed in the home, the undertaker would hang a floral wreath outside by the front door. People who would visit would sometimes bring some food and jugs of wine and spend time in and about the tenement with the grieving family. The old timer (the Italian) was in the burly Lebanese's kitchen when young Nichols and his father arrived. They chatted briefly.

The somber and sober old man agreed it was a tragedy…a pity…a piccata!!! And then he said something in Italian. "Il peggara per gusita, la angial per scaffica!!!" Nichols father seemed to understand, but not the young boy. When they left, the boy almost immediately asked his father what the old timer had said. Mr. Louie's father said, "Donato reminded me of an old saying from Italy…they always used to say it when someone young died…the ram for justice, the lamb for sacrifice."

Something is coming in on the wire…O*h Hell!!! Another one from the War Department*…he read the thin, lace-like strip of paper running off of the ticker tape…*I hope not...please God not again*!!! Mr. Louie kept reading the wire, and at the same time he expertly arranged the long ribbon paper message. The ticker tape continued to chatter and just as suddenly as it started, it stopped. Because of what he had just read, he thought the silence was deafening. He took a breath, with his right hand pulled off his eyeglasses from his face and rubbed his eyes with his left hand…*I can not change this …this was his destiny!!!*

- - A ram for Justice; A lamb for Sacrifice - -

Out loud, in a tired but firm voice (because he had to be in control now) he called out, "John please cut and paste this…the follow-up will be coming through in a minute…confirm receipt when it comes in…cut and paste it and then file the confirmation in today's packet. Who is available to make a bicycle delivery…Henry???…tell him to see me before he leaves…and John...get me Our Lady of Mt. Carmel's phone number at the rectory…I would like to speak to Father Pizzoglio…Thank you."

"Yes…Father Pizzoglio please…Padre this is Nick Louie…I am good thank you and how are you???…Padre, we got some bad news for one of your parishioners…Parteleo…they live at 846 Catherine…that's by the school isn't it???…the Melchiorre house you say??? How should we handle this one??? Okay…I'll have the boy wait for you before making the delivery…Good…and thank you…Oh padre", he hesitated, "Padre", he hesitated again...maybe a second longer than before, he sighed and said "…one more thing…tell that poor mother I am sorry…so very sorry for her loss."

God...??? ***Yes…Nichols what do you want???*** *I'm...I'm not sure...but I know I need You!!!* ***For what???*** *I'm not sure...but*...a long pause…*I need your help...* ***For what??? For what Nick…for what??? Come on Nicky…I'm busy…I got mankind to run and exploding stars in our universe…I'm busy…whaddya want???*** *Don't be mad at me...I'm just not sure...not sure...not sure*...his voice faded to almost a whisper…***Come on …come on Nicky…try…try to tell Me!!! What is it???…*** *God, why should I really care about that Italian woman or her wine drinking husband and her young son...what is he???...Eighteen, nineteen years old...bleeding and dying on some sandy beach in Okinawa...why should I want her know that I'm sorry...so very sorry for her loss??? Why???*

And God just rocked his head to the right and then to the left, half closed his eyes and half smiled and said…***Nick…Nick…I gotta remind you again??? It is because you are better…much better than a crocodile…a sea gull…a rat…a gorilla…a mule…a small donkey that***

pulls a loaded coal car with a blanket over his head and eyes…better than a squawking blue jay…you are better than just being the highest on the food chain…what makes you better??? It is your conscience…you are better…and don't you forget it!!!

The Western Union delivery boy got off of Genesee Street and pedaled straight over Catherine Street…right by the school he was told…*there!!! There it is…gotta be it …846...yeah this it!!!*

Mr. Louie's office furnished the boys with a military style officer's cap when making deliveries. The office only had two such Western Union hats; one very, very small and the other very, very large. Henry opted for the very large one even though he had to use his ears to keep it from falling over his forehead and into his eyes. He wore it way back on his head when he peddled the bike down Catherine Street.

The pastor of Our Lady of Mt Carmel was waiting on the front porch of the Melchiorre house when Henry got there. He was there with a young seminarian and Soura Anna Maria, the mother superior at their convent.

The biker propped his victory bike with the skinny tires against the stoop, took his oversize hat off (gladly), tucked it under his right armpit and said, "Father, Mr. Louie told me that I should go with you to make this delivery." Father Pizzoglio nodded yes.

The foursome entered the front door and climbed the front staircase to the third landing. Father Pizzoglio led the procession, followed by Mother Superior, Henry (his military cap still clamped firmly under his right armpit) and finally the shy seminarian.

The good pastor knocked on the screen door and when Maria Parteleo stepped away from the kitchen sink to see who it was, he asked in a tone of voice so very much different than the fire and brimstone and pleadings for a special collection you heard on Sunday mornings,

"Permisso???" And then, "Signora Parteleo, sono io Padre Pizzoglio e Suora Anna Maria e due altri."

As soon as she recognized the pastor, she quickly wiped her hands on her apron wondering if she should take it off quickly before receiving the guests or leave it on, she opted to leave it on and not have such distinguished people kept waiting. With both hands, she quickly smoothed her black hair…it now had a white streak in it that started just above the temple on the right side. She hurried to open the door.

"Avanti!!! Avanti!!! Monsignore…per la mora di Dio!!!" There were certain areas of southern Italy where the peasants (mostly the women and very young boys) always addressed any priest…especially a pastor...as Monsignore (My Lord) regardless of his status in the church. It would be another fifty…almost sixty…years before an Italian-America was made a Monsignor. The Diocese of Syracuse was, and probably still is, very Irish.

They all stood around the kitchen between the sink with the glass door cupboards overhead and the coal burning stove. The pastor cleared his throat and quietly told the mother that maybe she should sit down. Confused and wondering, she dutifully obeyed…*for the love of God...a pastor in my house…what an honor!!!*

Father Pizzoglio nodded to Henry. The young boy with a hat under his armpit, reached into his vest pocket, withdrew a yellowish envelope and slowly handed it to her. She did not understand…she did not know…

Pg Dn

Tony was up in Utica again and it was cold. He was driving and his truck heater seemed to roar and try hard to give some heated comfort. He was on his way to Goomba Joe's… right down Catherine Street. He decided to go that way because he wanted to see the old homestead at 912 and he was only at the 800 block. *Boy!!! Look at this shit!!! You won't know it was the same neighborhood...look at it!!! Just look at it!!!* he told himself. He slowed down and finally stopped and parked 'Big Green', his pickup truck.

He parked on the south side of the street at about the center of the old Brandegee School. Now it is Brandegee Apartments and it is totally fenced; a seven foot cyclone wraps the entire property, save maybe two separate side by side double gate entrances on the Jay Street side and one double gate on the Catherine street side. When he was a kid, the only fence ran from Catherine Street to Jay Street on the far west property line. It separated the schoolyard from the private property of the Melchiorre House, with its long garbage shed in back. There was another barn/garage that faced Jay Street. Tony remembered there was a little candy store located in a smaller front portion of a two-story frame residence also facing Jay Street. *They are gone...all gone!!!*

Already in a melancholy mood, he sensed that it was all going to be depressing...this stopping and looking for the past and some ghost.

He sighed, reached for a DiNapoli and a box of wooden matches. He reminded himself that this was the only way to light up a good Tuscany cigar. The ritual of rotating the cigar and at the same time twisting the flaming matchstick guaranteed a good light. The cab filled with bluish gray smoke as Tony 'snapped' the flame off of the matchstick, cranked the window down an inch or two, and threw out the burnt matchstick.

Not as many stacks of cement block skyscrapers (the little kids used to call them that*) lining the fence line...and the double cylinder concrete towers look as beat up and as dusty as dey used ta be...*Tony studied them and wanted to smile, but could not, he turned his head and looked at the Brandegee Apartments, the main entrance is on Jay Street.

He thought about that for a second because at this late stage in his life, he could not remember which or what was the main entrance when it was a school. He remembered the Boys entrance and the Girls entrance…*and…and…dare…up dare in da middle of the reddish bricks used to be a big gray finished cement batch dat said BOYS…dare right in the middle of the long part of the old building between Catherine and Jay street…going towards Kossuth…the girls door was on the Jay Street side...down like an alley…because dats where the old building 'teed' into the new building...*

Tony kind of reached and stretched his neck to see if he could find or see the gray cement patch that seemed to yell "Boys"….he couldn't…not from where he was parked. The lettering was all in caps, he always remembered that. He looked to his front.

The Melchiorre House is long gone, as are the other two three-decker frame tenements. Empty lots…with a junked car there and about four grocery store shopping carts scattering the desolate landscape. Marraffa's fish market is still there and prospering with (what Tony was told by his mother) a Sicilian family that came to America in the fifties running it.

From his parked truck, Tony saw a much different perspective of the market than he remembered. He nodded to himself and thought…*Paint job looks fairly recent, looks well maintained...wonder where they stack their garbage on garbage day...dat telephone pole is still there.*

Tony turned the ignition key and the pickup loudly responded. Time to go to Goomba Joe's. He shifted into second and then third gears and soon glided by the first vacant lot, where the old Melchiorre House used to stand.

As he passed it, he turned slightly because he thought he may have heard a wailing or a moaning cry coming from that vacant weedy lot.

It was nothing. He did notice however, none of the abandoned shopping carts had wheels on them, and he wasn't surprised. Tony knew that in Belize it would not be just the wheels missing.

The Ripple Effect

Pg Up

When they all first heard that blood curdling scream, nine year old Angela Melchiorre was in the kitchen with her mother, her younger brother and youngest sister. Ma Melchiorre's immediate reaction was predictable, prompt and direct; she knew…as all mothers seem to know…she was needed…somewhere…and would not run away from the screams, but toward them.

Ma quickly instructed Angie to stay in the kitchen, watch her sister and to only leave if she sends for her. In the same breath, she ordered her son to go outside and play in the schoolyard and…don't cross the street!

She then disappeared into the hallway and Angela heard her and others rushing up the front staircase. Stout, sturdy, strong women…still in aprons…climbing up...up to where they were needed.

Little Angela stayed in the center of the kitchen for a moment very frightened and confused because she did not totally understand what was going on. She then noticed that her little sister was frightened and on the verge of tears. Angie tried to gain control of her fears…half succeeded…and went directly to her little sister to calm her and tell her everything was going to be alright. Even at the age of nine, that young girl knew the youngest must be protected.

...I am only going to the screen door to see if I can see what is happening…

She pushed the screen door open just a little bit…and the first thing she saw was a frightened looking young boy almost running down the staircase. He was putting a soldier-like round cap upon his head, tucked firmly as if he was worried the wind would blow it off. He was running when he got to the front door, he jumped onto his bike and pedaled off toward and then past Brandegee School.

When Henry went home that night, he asked his mom if it was alright to quit his job at Western Union. "Really Henry? I thought you like it so much is there something wrong? Why in the world do you want to leave?" He explained and his mother...almost as if they were in church...sobbed a tearless sob and quietly said, "Old dear," and with those two words and with all the grieving understanding of a sympathetic mother...she tenderly embraced her son and she held him close to her heart.

La Signora Parteleo's youngest son, with his flashing jet black eyes and his curly hair and his happy disposition...that quick...friendly and sometime teasing smile...was dead. He had died on a desolate piece of land in the middle of the ocean far, far away in a land called Okinawa.

The Ripple Effect

A ripple within a ripple within a ripple

A female rat was climbing up the side of a garbage can behind the locked doors of the long gray garbage shed. Her ears perked quickly, she sensed the fatality of the sound and pitch of the scream. She immediately dropped to the dirt floor of the shed and scurried quickly to her nest, her young were there. An emaciated calico cat, slowly walking on the second floor landing, who had the week before secretly delivered a litter of six, stopped dead in her tracks...she recoiled and took two paces back, she looked up with frightened eyes at where the sound came from. She, too, scurried back to her basement nursery, by one of the tenant's coal bin, her young were there.

The two large male dogs on the other side of the fish market's counter, by the big black National Cash

Register…lifted and turned their heads toward Brandegee School. They sniffed the air, ears perked they heard the second screech and cocked their heads with a curious look on their faces. They waited a second and then just put their heads down on their paws and continued to sleep: on the other side of the counter…by the big black National Cash register.

A flock of pigeons who were roosting high up on top of the twin N.D. Peters concrete silos and its gray dust covered control shed...way up there at the top…which housed the pulleys and cables that lifted and then dropped both stone and powdered cement to a vertical chute and the construction material would plunge downwards into the huge drum of the idling cement mixer, also heard the first and second scream.

Long before the circular rippling sound waves of the first ebbed, the birds were in flight led by a hen who felt she had to return to her nest with two eggs. They all fluttered upward and circled and dove and swirled high above the construction yard and its stack of cement blocks and high above Brandegee School's long flat roof. In reality, it seemed…maybe because it WAS…only one of those frantic pigeons knew where it was going and the others only tended to disorient her and get in her way.

The loosely packed flock of hundreds of pigeons swirled and twisted and dove and climbed like a finely choreographed and rehearsed ballet. The color, mostly white, did have hints of bluish gray and light gray flashing here and there in a chilly blue sky of East Utica.

The chickens running around in the 'back' courtyard of Marraffa's Fish and Poultry Market, were squawking and in a different wild frenzy; they had discovered one of their own, had an open wound and blood was showing. Before too long, the squawking and cackling chickens would peck unmercifully at the open wound, pecking the wounded bird to death. It was one of their very own...that very soon lay motionless in the middle of the courtyard. One of their own.

A Melancholy Refrain

They say that la Signora Parteleo was never ever really the same after that fateful May afternoon. Her youngest son, with his flashing jet black eyes and his curly hair and his happy disposition...that quick...friendly and sometimes teasing smile...was dead. He had died on a piece of land in the middle of the ocean far, far away called Okinawa.

Console the Grieving

Pg Dn

Tony had just finished planting the last of his tomato plants, and they were late in getting in this year, it was the first ten days of July already. But they are in, *thank God*, and in spite of the foul weather, his garden was finally complete. *It is a bitch getting up and down!!! Christ I wish my legs didn't bother me so much...getting old sucks!!!*

He took another break. He hobbled into his screened in porch, sat and poured himself a glass of wine and then…like a religious ritual…lit up a Tuscany cigar. He watched the bluish gray smoke billow, begin to dissipate and then disappear altogether.

He relaxed. It was all there, his bird bath, the arbor, the huge maple and smaller pear (both planted on the same day), the back garden and the fig tree; all present and accounted for. He puffed on his cigar again and then lazily turned his head to follow the expanding smoke cloud. There!!!...there on the other side of the fountain and the white picket cedar fence and the arborvitaes shrubs…a minor 'nature type' ruckus was developing.

A big black crow had landed on his neighbor's shrub…he didn't know the type or name of it…but it loses its leaves in the winter. He took another sip from his wine glass and watched.

Within minutes…no, seconds…much smaller black birds (*Starlings??? He didn't know that either*), dove and squawked and pulled up and dove again at the big crow. The crow hopped from branch to branch, and then disappeared into the thicket of the shrub, re-emerged with something pinkish/brownish in its beak and took off to open space. The starlings…now six in number…all squawking, banked and twisted and gave chase. The crow pumped what appeared to be much bigger and more powerful wings, gained altitude rapidly and gracefully disappeared.

That bastard!!! It raided a nest and took a fledgling!!!

Somehow, it reminded Tony of something long ago. *How different are we from God's creatures??? Really!!! How different???* He thought. Later in the afternoon, and after several glasses of red wine and a finished cigar, Tony noticed a Robin on the same neighbor's shrub. It landed almost at the same spot the crow had. The Robin seemed to look around and then disappear into the thicket of the scrub. The Robin re-emerged too, and appeared to stay a little bit longer than necessary but then it too flew off.

Son of a bitch!!! Tony thought…*it was a Robin's nest the crow raided, but it was the starlings that tried to protect it.* Tony finally remembered what it all reminded him of earlier. He asked himself again…*how different are we from animals and God's creatures??*

The Chianti continued to do its work…deaden his senses, made him feel just a bit more relaxed and maybe melancholy. In this welcomed limbo and suspended mood, something in the back of his head just said…*'member the Parteleo family that lived in the Melchiorre house??*

Pg Up

It was a Friday. At about nine o'clock in the morning, Tony's mom left Aunt Grace at the bakery to wait on any customers and she would certainly be back by noon time to help wait on the midday crowd. They would then stay there at their assigned posts, by the National Cash Register and the bread racks, until well after the three-thirty whistles from the mills…and remain there sometimes as late as five-thirty.

It was Ma's turn (the sisters would alternate weekly) to go to Arcuri & Marangi's Meat Market on

Bleecker Street and she wanted to leave early because she had an obligation to fulfill. Zia Grazia understood.

The butcher shop was located in the middle of that very long and crowded 600 block of Bleecker, next to Malaria's Record Shop. The store was across the street from Goomba Giovanni's shoe repair store…Goomba Giovanni and his wife stood as Godparents to Tony. If the Goomba was outside or by the window of his shop they would wave to each other and exchange a greeting. His shop was on the south side of Bleecker, and Dominick Marangi's Meat Market was on the north side. Dominick's wife and Goomba Giovanni's wife were sisters, and from the same village as Tony's father, Cisternino. Their husbands, however, were from le Pulgia, but not Cisternino: one was from Aberobella, the other from Locorontondo. Tony learned all these things growing up and being by his mother and aunts; before he went to school and learned. *You interpret learning however you like.*

Ma was going to the meat market to order the weekly supply of meats for the families. Ma and Zia Grazia and sometimes Zia Lucia and Zia Grace (Uncle Mike's American born wife) took turns going to the meat market. They did it this way for several reasons; not only to give the buyer a much stronger bartering position (and nobody could *Jew 'em* down better than Zia Grazia) but also to *'see'* the quality, the freshness and texture of the meats that were sold. Zia Grazia, sometimes, would even insist upon smelling the meat; she was tough. Tony's Ma was not as boisterous or flamboyant, but she was effective with a little tip of the head, looking at the bottom of her nose…bobbing her head "NO" at the cost...twitching her nose…she got the job done without too much showmanship.

Dominick would rip a small piece of the sort of faded orange (not bright orange) colored wrapping paper from the horizontal roll (only about five inches) and place it by the cone of string used to wrap the meats. This would become his tally sheet: the ground meat (divided in half or thirds, etc), the broacsoli, the liver, spare ribs, eight or ten soup bones. “Eay!!! Per l’amore de Dio!!! (For the love of God) leave some meat on it!!!” And so it went. He would take an order, cut it if necessary, and wrap it in the slightly waxy orangish colored paper. With the years of experience showing, he’d wrap the parcel. He’d then pull the pencil from the back of his earlobe, lick the tip of it, and mark both the parcel and his tally sheet. He ran his grand total on the orangish strip of wrapping paper. He would price each cut and wrap it, and the woman would do ‘their’ math, which may not necessarily coincide with what the big butcher, with his white apron and white circular paper hat, put down on the bundle. If you asked either, they would simply say it was their way of maintaining a friendship. Whoever went that week would pay in cash then and there, trading the money for his tally sheet.

Dominick and his partner, Arcuri, liked doing business with Tony’s family. They were regular, dependable (always buying something) and loyal customers…going back to those hard days when he would want to charge a nickel for a big soup bone and take two cents instead. Further, they were piasanos and goombas.

About three-thirty, the kids would come home from school, each family included in the meat supply purchase would send one or more of the kids to pick up the individually packed parcels. The eldest was in charge of the money…to the penny!!! Tony and DeeBee and Joe would often recall and remember those Friday afternoon trips to Arcuri & Marangi, and taking those (what then seemed like such very heavy) bundles of meats back to the bakery.

Each matriarch took their supply home that night. *You don’t ever, never eat meat on Friday because the priest and nuns at Saint Ant-knee say so!!! But even worser dan dat…Ma and Pa and every else sez so…never ever…you could go to hell if you didn't get to confession before you die...to hell!!!* The meat was sometimes unwrapped, if the paper wasn't soiled, it would be folded and stored for future use. The strings used in the wrapping of the parcels, were untangled if necessary and tied to the string ball in the cupboard drawer. It was important that you tied an end of the new string to the end of the last string in the ball. Wind the new string around and around...*Look at dat!!! Almost as big as a softball with lots and lots of electric tape wrapped around it.* The girls would probably say a grapefruit. Like a calendar picture of the Sacred Heart of Jesus, every house had at least one string ball.

This day, Ma left the butcher shop and went up Bleecker to Hubbel, turned right, then left on Jay and walked to Kossuth. She wanted to take this route because she hoped the kids would be out at recess (she would always quietly smile and remember her earlier carefree days)...and...and...pulling herself back to today's harsh realities. She wanted to stop at Trevesani's and buy a small bag of fruit. She had an obligation to perform.

Ma also purchased a half dozen eggs and exited Tony Marraffa's fish and poultry store. She stood, just a second, on the sidewalk at Catherine and Kossuth, not that she was tired, but in a melancholy...saddening...mood, remembering a few minutes ago children running and playing and laughing in the near-by schoolyard. At this corner she thought, for no apparent reason, this is the dividing line between Our Lady of Mt Carmel and St. Anthony's parishes...but we all are Catholics. Ma went to the Melchiorre House and climbed the two flights of stairs to the third floor front apartment. Next door, the kids had left the schoolyard, recess was over. And Ma thought*, che croce*...What a cross.

She had come to pay her individual respects to the Parteleo family and especially Maria...the grieving mother. She found one of the Parteleo girls at home and Maria sitting by the kitchen window on the far end of the room. Ma gave the little gifts she had purchased to the Parteleo girl. The girl thanked her and then offered her a chair by her grieving mother. (The small food gift goes back to the vizza (customs) of the old country, especially in an agrarian society.) The ladies visited for a few minutes, and when it was time to leave, Ma kissed the grieving mother on both cheeks. Both Maria and Ma just slightly tasted…if at all…maybe just only sensed…the salty taste of each other's tears. Everyone knows tears, and blood, are equally salty.

As Ma descended the staircases, all she could think of was *che croce che croce*…What a cross, what a cross!!! Even though she walked slowly with a heavy heart, she made it back to the bakery in ample time, about a quarter after eleven.

Zia Grazia just looked at her sister, who had three sons, and knew what she was thinking, and for the longest time said nothing. Zia Grazia also knew the obligation that Ma had seen to. Finally, and before the school lunch bell sounded at noon, she quietly asked, "Come sta Maria?" (How is Maria?).

There was a long pause. Zia Grazia sensed that Ma was struggling. Her eyes seemed to be getting more watery and Ma finally answered, "Non hai trovato buon…io mei credo che commara Maria non stai per noi tanto a sigia". (I did not find her well; I believe that Maria won't be with us too much longer.) It had confirmed Zia Grazia's earlier observations and she just clucked and hooded her eyes for a moment.

American Legion Visit

Pg Up

Tony would describe it as "a funny thing" that happened the other day. And he would tell you, he and his wife went to his daughter's house to babysit the four grandkids. His daughter and son-in-law had a dinner date and it so happened they were running late. He and his wife (his wife more so) tried to be helpful…his wife getting the kids into their pajamas, making sure they brushed their teeth, as his own daughter scurried about. Finally, as they were leaving, his son-in-law came back into living room to remind Tony of a detail that Tony was already aware of…and in an offhand, wise-ass reply, Tony said, "Yeah!!! Yeah!!! I know…I know…get your ass out of here, get going!"

They left.

Tony turned and started to head upstairs to the bedrooms and was surprised to see his oldest granddaughters both standing in the archway at the foot of the staircase. They both looked shocked and saddened. He noticed it right away and inquired, "Hey kids…you look mad…what's wrong?" "Why did you tell my daddy to get out?" And the other, "Why did you use a bad word?" Tony explained that he was only trying to help and make sure their parents got to the dinner on time. The little girls accepted his honest explanation…but in a sense…he could not forgive himself…and he was very sorry that he hurt their feelings. *Whadda big ugly mouth you got!*

Pg Up

Some weeks after the family was notified, but before the remains of Jerry
Parteleo were returned to his family, a contingent from the American Legion Post

1234 called at their tenement flat one late Sunday afternoon. They found the two Parteleo girls at the kitchen having some biscotti and Medalia d'Oro black coffee in demitasse cups with their small saucers and even tinier spoons. They had already cleared, cleaned and put away all the dishes and pots and pans.

Pa had gone to pay his condolences to a close friend whose mother died in Italy; news like that in those days was always relayed via the church.

Ma was sitting by the kitchen window looking out over the schoolyard. She sat quietly, with both hands holding the Rosary. But Ma wasn't praying she was just staring out over the schoolyard and onto Catherine Street and a small portion of the N.D. Peter's Construction Yard. She seldom blinked and just stared out at her American landscape, occasionally thinking of the mountains of Calabria.

Her eldest daughter, who was to be married as soon as her man got out of the navy, was starting to worry more and more about her Ma's mental health. *Oh No God...No, No God!!! Not the crazy house...not the crazy house...Utica State Hospital way over on the west side...not the crazy house... please God let her get better give us a sign just a little sign PLEASE!!!* She continued to bite her lower lip her younger sister noticed her anguish and quietly started to weep.

A knock on the screen…it was more of a rattle than a sharp knock or rap…"Yes?? Who is it???"

"Do Mr. and Mrs. Gerald Parteleo live here???" "Yes!!!" Of course...everyone in the neighborhood knew that! But, the men at the door where not from the neighborhood.

"My name is John something and this is Robert something else and I am the President of the American Legion Post 1234 and Bob here is Sergeant of Arms." A pause and the sisters looked at one another then back to the men standing on the threshold of their five room cold water flat. What in the world would they want here?

John, the President of Post 1234, noted the silence and confused looks, cleared his throat and continued. "We understand that the Parteleo family has (and he realized at once his choice of the word "has" may not be appropriate and quickly said) had three sons serving in the armed forces. We are sorry to hear of your recent loss, but understand one of the boys will be getting discharged soon…he is at Rhodes Hospital…I am told…is that right? And they tell me he'll be home soon…the other is in the Philippines and is safe and doing well I understand. Are you ladies their sisters??" "Yes we are." "Is that your mother at the window??" Yes it was…

"We would like to present a little something to show our appreciation, may we??" The sisters again looked at one another and not really knowing what to do, they nodded their approval.

The four of them, in single file, walked across the largest room in the flat, the eldest daughter leading, the President of Post 1234, the Sergeant at Arms and the youngest daughter. When they got to the seated matriarch, they fanned out around her.

Still seated, she looked up at them; she looked at the strangers, then at her daughters, her eyes begging for an explanation or introduction from them. She did not know these men, who look like they never smile, she never saw them, but *maybe…maybe they will bring my Jerry home…oh God please…!!!*

"Mrs. Parteleo on behalf of the American Legion Post 1234 my I present to you this small window banner as to enable you to show the outside world that you have made a great sacrifice for America." The banner was like a Chinese calendar that comes rolled on a stick. And, like a Roman scroll, the president of Post 1234 carefully unrolled the banner. It was bordered in red, it was rectangular, and inside the red border was a, pure as the fresh driven snow, field of white; and in the center and lengthwise were three stars. In a geometrically perfect row and upon that field of white silk bordered by red, laid three stars, the top and bottom stars were dark blue and the one star in the middle was gold…

Since neither of the two American Legion officers were as sensitive or as wise or as understanding or as good as Mr. Louie, the Sergeant at Arms made a regrettable error in sensitivity. It was his misfortune that the President of Post 1234 did see what was about to happen but did nothing. Maybe too…the Saints in Heaven above could have saved both of them, but somehow, they did not intervene.

The Sergeant at Arms thought that the poor woman staring out the kitchen window did not understand nor appreciate their noble gesture; she probably could not speak any English anyway! (*What the hell...she lived in this dumpy cold water flat and this entire neighborhood is full of guineas anyway...how could she talk **American** like us!!!)*

He started to explain to the grieving mother what a great honor it was to have a son give his life for the Country. How proud she must be and how proud the boys at Post 1234 were to present this banner to remind her that the Gold Star in the center was for her son…"Yes George"… (the president touched his elbow and whispered in his ear) "I mean Jerry died a hero for the good old red white and blue! You see this gold star…it is for your Jerry!"

Ma maybe didn't speak perfect English, but over the years she did pick up a bit…and certainly the word Jerry was a word she knew. The Sergeant at Arms gently laid the small window banner on her lap and pointed to the gold star and repeated, "Jerry…Your Jerry!!!"

That small window banner and the words of this stranger…who was speaking in what he though was understandable but very false broken Italian-English, like they did on the radio…was telling her that banner with the gold star was an honor a thing to cherish. But to that little frail woman, the star and the banner was as heavy as Jesus Christ was on His Mother's lap in Michelangelo's sculpture masterpiece, the Pieta.

What happened next no one there in that cold water flat or anywhere else in the Old Melchiorre House will ever forget. La Signora Parteleo shattered that Sunday afternoon serene calm, she screamed that screeching wounded animal cry that echoed in the hallways of the tenement down into the alleyways of the neighborhood, over the skyscraping stack of cement blocks in the construction yard, bouncing off of the reddish brick walls of Brandegee School and thumbing out over to Jay Street and Broad Street.

The Sergeant at Arms was never so shocked in all his life, and wondered why the old lady dressed from head to toe in black, acted like that. The President of Post 1234 was just as surprised and thought *maybe...possibly Bob should not have stressed the gold star so much…then again maybe not…that old lady maybe a nutso!!!*

Had a hidden cherry bomb firecracker suddenly exploded in their face at that instant, the President of the American Legion Post 1234 and the Sergeant at Arms of the American Legion Post 1234 could not have been more shocked...surprised, and yes...more frightened…than what was caused by that shrilling scream of mother, who till then, was just sitting quietly by her kitchen window. She did not want a window banner with a gold star in the center, she wanted her baby Gennaro. *I wish this man who is speaking to me with such nonsense…and silly words…I don't understand him…I don't want him in my house or in my face…I want him to go far away…I want my little my little Jerry…I want him in my house…I want my little Jerry.*

It seemed her daughters were at her side before the circular sound ripples reached the screen door. "It is okay Ma it is okay…don't cry…please don't cry...they don't mean any harm…they don't understand…it'll be all right! Don't cry Ma…please don't cry."

A split second later, the youngest turned and faced the very surprised men whose eyes were wide and unblinking and terrified and whose mouths just dropped open. Her neck and head seemed to shrink into her shoulders and her shoulders expanded like a cobra, ready.

She hissed, just a pitch above a church whisper, and started to move slowly forward as if a cobra ready to strike and destroy and devour, and said, "You rotten son of a bitch…you heartless bastard…see what you've done? With your stupid broken accent...trying to be what you are not! Or, ever will be…you bastard!"

The Sergeant at Arms and the post President were walking slowly backwards as if possessed by the movement of a snake charmer…still very terrified. Angie's mother was racing up the stairs…Philomena Leone was already entering the kitchen…Annie Lo Conto right behind her…"What happened? Who are these men…your mother alright? You kids all right…Angelo come up here…what happened…Nichole vain a qua (Nick come here) these men hurt you?"

"What? What? What in the world did we do, what?"

The questions of innocence, ignorance neither appeased nor slowed down the deadly advance of the hooded cobra. She suddenly started to speak and curse in Italian…still hissing. "Possa fa na vomicata de sange! Lurido bastardo!" (You should vomit blood you rotten bastard.)

The President and the Sergeant were still walking backwards. When in the corridor of the tenement, still wild eyed confused and beginning to be taken over by the animal instinct to run from danger, they turned on their heels and started their dash down the two flights. They passed Angie's mother (still in her apron) halfway on the second staircase...and not really knowing why, other than the tranquility of that Sunday afternoon was disturbed and these strangers must have been responsible, she said in her best but broken English, "Goa awaya! Goa awaya! Vatina. Vatina." (Go away...go away...get out...get out)

Neither the President nor the recently elected Sergeant at Arms needed to be told as they practically tumbled down the staircase. At the head of the final staircase...and their safety, they met Nicole who was responding to his wife's and Angie mother's call...from the pitch the men in the tenement knew something was askew. He did not know what was going on, but something told him these running men were responsible and women were calling for help and he had to go to their side first. For good measure, he threw his elbow into the President's rib cage as they rushed past him on the staircase, but missed because he was a tad too late for the Sergeant at Arms. Also responding was Angie's father, a burly construction worker and for all the same reasons that had motivated his neighbor, he did the same, but missed neither. However, for some reason or other when he elbowed the second larger man, he did it with more speed, more authority and as much force of an angry section boss. He cursed the *somana beech!!!*

The screeching woman in black sitting by her kitchen window, the hissing daughter defiantly facing him down, the women in aprons arriving at the screen door, the flight down the stairs, the elbows in the rib was just too much for the President. His fingers were trembling when he, at last, reached his car and he tried to put the key into the ignition of his two passenger business coupe, he didn't feel safe yet and was trying to tell the Sergeant at Arms to hurry but could not speak aloud. The engine roared, the Sergeant was closing his door and the automobile rapidly left the curb in front of the Melchiorre House, right next to the Brandegee Schoolyard.

Back safe and sound in the walls of Post 1234, both men quick stepped to the bar and ordered a couple of stiff drinks. The President who was a dental assistant when he served from September 1917 thru December of 1918, at Fort Dix for the entire duration slammed the first one down and told Zarb the bartender "Gimme a nudder!!! Quick!!!"

The Sergeant at Arms, who a few minutes ago was telling a heart broken woman…it was an honor to lose a son for the country, was also shaken. His military contribution was fourteen and a half months in Alabama somewhere repairing canvas for field tents.

In time however, and after a couple more shooters, his bravado returned and he was telling the other bar patrons about this crazy old Dago lady dressed from head to toe in black screaming like hell when he just gently laid the small silky window banner on her lap. "Jesus Christ!!! You'd think I dropped a hundred pounds of potatoes on her lap…Nutso guinea!!!"

Nobody laughed although he thought it was funny. Four members of Post 1234 at the far end of the bar, drained their glass and said, "See ya later Zarb", but said nothing whatsoever to either the President or the Sergeant at Arms. "What's buggin those guys???" asked the Sergeant at Arms loud enough to be heard throughout the barroom of Post 1234.

Although Big Zarb was half Syrian and half Polish, he looked more Mediterranean than his siblings. He was dark skinned, not as tall as his brothers, but much wider. To see him would be living proof that muscle did indeed weigh more than fat. He was an ex-Marine and served in France and often bragged that his only claim to fame was that one of the companies in his Regiment was that of Master Sergeant Dan Daily. He never would say he fought along side of Sgt. Daily, but would admit he marched in the same parades.

Zarb wiped his hands after having finished rinsing beer mugs, hung the towel by the beer taps, looked forlornly at the ceiling and then walked down to where some of the real and understanding heroes were still sitting. He looked first at the President and then to his drinking companion, and quietly said, “John you either get this asshole out of the room or find a new bartender.”

Looking For Something Better

Pg Dn

It was in Belize and it wasn't that long ago. It was Tony's first Caribbean cruise; they left out of Tampa, Florida. Tony was always a chowhound, and…no surprise…he drank too much. But, he wasn't much on large boats and open sea, not since that February, North Atlantic crossing so long ago. Looking back, it wasn't that bad, but it was still a merchant marine run troop ship, and the seas got choppy, and sometimes you had to eat standing up…those long tables in the galley were adjustable for that very purpose. That was the Buckner. Coming back on the Butner was in May and the seas not as choppy. Tony secretly feared the open water…the ocean…it was like an imbedded tombstone…somewhere very deep in his gut…*that* inner fear that you knew…felt and dreaded…that any incident would be fatal…no getting out of it. And from the womb of the troop carrier, all you would see was water, today and yesterday, and you'd see water the day after and the day after that, water…only water.

But a cruise, and a cruise ship, were different in every way he could think of… and remember. The size of the vessel really impressed him, more than he thought it would. Sure he'd seen cruise ships on television and in the movies, but…*God!!! This thing is enormous!* Looked like twice as many people than the Butner had on board with the 26th Infantry. Each passenger had a bed or a double bed, a room (Cabin) or a suite, an efficient and compact lavatory with instant hot water and maid service, a TV and elevator music piped in if you so desired. And the chow was there three times a day, and the 'Lido Deck' a continuously open galley, and…and enough booze to drown an elephant.

Tony smirked to himself as though no one noticed; but she did. She asked why and he told her he was thinking of an old Mel Brooks movie where an actor states, "It is good to be King." And then he said, "You and me kid are gunna live like Kings and Queens for the next week, or ten days, or whatever, this is great. That and we got hundreds of people running around whose only job is to make us happy."

His wife had signed up to go ashore for a tour of Belize…which Tony had recently been advised was once called British Honduras (he recognized that name). They were going all together, the group that they had made the trip with and good friends from home. A tender took them to shore, and soon enough, the girls organized a bus tour of the countryside.

A day or so after the excursion to Belize and the cruise liner was again out to sea…and when Tony found himself alone...alone in a crowd…looking at the Caribbean from a comfortable bar stool. A Sailor would call it in the 'aft' and not the stern, (but *who was a sailor?).* Tony's eyes squinted a bit and dark memories, unwanted memories... flashed across his mind like a roll of paper unwinding. The sea mesmerized him, and in his half drunken stupor he remembered a cold Monday morning in November and an even colder January afternoon by Uncle Joe's bakery, a zillion years ago. He could take you there today…both places and show exactly where he was standing so many, many years ago. He sipped some more Grappa, hooded his eyes…almost closing them…and shook his head like he just gotten an icy chill. *Don't go there you big goof!!! It ain't smart…you don't need to drag that grief out again*…but he did not heed his own advice he thought…*Getting drunk again huh??? But what the Hell??? It is paid for!!!...It is, indeed, good to be King.*

I see women on bended knee...cut cane for the family…

I see men against sea casting nets at the surging tide…

Lyrics from 'Island in the Sun'...recorded by Harry Bellefonte.

The tour bus in Belize drove up a country road and soon, there was an old cemetery on the right and a large city dump on the left. A zillion sea gulls were squawking and screeching and circling overhead, occasionally diving down. *Whadda ya doin here??? Get out!!! This is mine...get the hell out of here!!!* The target??

Tony saw two women bending over...almost at a right angle...rummaging the surroundings and about four or five children (slightly behind them) just rumpling around. The dump soil was as black as sin and was contrasted by the white and gray sea gulls, but what made the ground sinisterly black were the discarded plastic shopping bags strewn and blowing about.

Good to be king, as Tony remembered an old movie line; and in an instant he also remembered, what to him, was very dark thought...and added...if you don't have to pick garbage.

Pg Up

Frustrated with that large stupid soft spot in that stupid little pumpkin....right smack in the middle of it...trying to carve it...*try to make two small eyes...but the nose is too big...I hadda cut out dat rotten part.* He was hiding it from other kids...hiding it from Ma and Aunt Grace...it is dirty and filthy to touch garbage let alone covet it...he was on the side porch...second floor rear...*What??? Dat somebody coming up the stairs??? Quick hide the pumpkin...dare!!! Under dat box...*(an old 42lb grape box)...*Quick!!!...turn it upside down...hide it...hide it!! What would people say if they found ya trying to carve a Halloween pumpkin after Thanksgiving??? Halloween was a long time ago!!! Quick hide it...HIDE*

*IT!!! Whadda goof you are!!! Trying to carve a jack-o-lantern so late...but...but...**I never** had a jack-o-lantern...ever!!!*

They didn't go to school the day after Thanksgiving and Tony found the rotten pumpkin in Tony Maraffa's garbage pile, on the southeast corner of Catherine Street and Kossuth Avenue. The city garbage collectors were running late due the heavy holiday volume. Tony found the discarded pumpkin in an old orange crate, half buried under rotting cabbage leaves. He unbuttoned his hooded parka, rescued the pumpkin with his right hand, and placed it in his coat right under his heart. Then, cradling his new treasure with his left arm outside the parka, looked around, and then ran home. Only God saw him take it.

Then there was a blue and white toy motor boat!!! *Whadda a beauty!!! Who da hell wood trow sumptin like dis a way?* Its 'aft' was sticking up out between two brown paper grocery bags filled with what could have been kitchen waste. Tony looked around quickly*...nobody...wasn't dat Joey's boat??? Didn't he get it just this past Christmas??? Did he break it all ready?* He pulled it out from between the two reused grocery bags and with a gleam in his eye, as well as wonderment for making such a find, he evaluated it. *Whats dat???* A red stain on the white underside...spit on it...wipe it with the back your sleeve...*GONE!!! Great...whadda find...nobody around...nobody...slip it under your coat...go home...you gotta find a good hiding place for it...under the bathtub*...four cast iron eagle claw talons supporting a heavy cast iron tub, with its enamel starting to show age...*nobody will ever look dere!!! Ma keeps that little blue and white basin dere...for when somebody is sick and throws up...*

The windshield is gone...*dats all right...God, I hope it floats...bet it'll float...itz gotta...dere no holes in the bottom of the motor boat.* Little Tony took it home and hid it. Only God saw him take it from the garbage barrel by Uncle Joe's bakery on Pelletieri Avenue. The garbage barrel stood by the telephone pole and right at the top of the curb.

It came to pass that Tony would play with and treasure this broken, disregarded blue and white toy motor boat. It did indeed float. Friday nights were bath nights, and Tony was always the first, his older brothers were usually outside playing and had to be called in. Ma left Tony alone, and allowed him to 'soak'.

They used to heat all their hot water in a tank located in the kitchen. Sometimes when Tony played on the floor, he would look up and imagine the hot water tank was a bomb…sometimes an upright torpedo…sometimes a snow covered mountain…Pa painted it with a silver colored enamel…*Sure!!! Dat could be snow!!!*

He loved those Friday evening baths…"*Antonio sei finuto…sei pronto???"* (Anthony are you done…are you ready to come out?) "Aww Ma…can't I stay for ten more minutes??? Don't forget ya gotta heat the water for Angelo and Sal…"

"Chia bassanto l'augua caldo…fa subito!!!" (I have enough hot water…hurry up.)

The imaginary PT boat captain would then step up and climb out of that high cast iron bathtub, supported by eagle talons, rescue his blue and white prize (returning it to a safe harbor) and start to dry himself. (He was first on the bath towel too.)

Nothing good lasts forever…nothing bad does either. Ma found the broken toy motor boat once when one of her boys was sick. She went to fetch that basin from underneath the tub and found it. She was too busy to start an inquisition and merely threw it away.

He loved the boat…hid it under the bathtub…with its four eagle claw feet…a safe harbor…the snow around him was white….not pitch black…with a scattering of pure white plastic bags…

Pg Dn

…and the snow around them…those bending women…looking like a broken match stick…was pure white…not pitch black.

The bouncing…skipping…trying to get airborne…disregarded plastic bags, aren't as pure white…maybe gray…like the sea gulls.

The seagulls…screaming and squawking and diving and shrilling…*get out get out...this is mine!!!...This is all mine!!!*

God Bless America

The Bulls
Pg Dn

His daughter was in college, one of his sons was stationed in Okinawa with the
Marines and the other had his home in west Allentown, and Tony and his wife, were in
Spain…Costa de Sol to be exact…on vacation.

It was in November, a Sunday, and it was raining on and off, and his wife had a horrendous head cold…and they only fought the bulls on Sunday afternoons. *Dats the main reason I let her talk me into going to Spain rather than It-Lee. What did Hemingway really see in bullfighting???* Tony often wondered especially after reading, *The Sun Also Rises.* He started early to campaign, coax, sweet talk, cajole his wife to go with him…"It's not that far…the guy at the front desk said the bus will take us there in less than fifteen minutes."

He continued his pleading, "We should be back way before six…it gets dark quick you know…and it is still November…you know how much I always wanted to see a real bull fight"…he sensed he was winning her over…"if we get therc early or get out early maybe you can do some shopping in the little bazaars they got in all these little village squares…dress warm…we got an umbrella…the bus comes to the front of the motel and drops you off in the center of the town…Come on…be a sport."

They got into the center of the mountain village and it was raining a little bit harder. They found a small cantina right next to a pottery shop, and she agreed to stop in with him and have a glass of wine…"maybe it'll warm you a bit."

They walked in and found a small table with two chairs by the wall and far enough away from the door to keep it cozy. It was dimly lit…*whaddya expect…you're in the mountains of Spain…*but not as damp…warmer…cozier…and friendlier and it all made you feel welcome. It pleased his wife too.

Tony ordered a carafe of local red wine. The owner returned with two glasses and the carafe. On a whim, Tony asked if they had any bread in the kitchen, the owner, once he understood Tony's request, he nodded yes, and disappeared into the back room. He retuned shortly…with a fresh, crusty…well cooked…half loaf of bread. Husband and wife…almost like a religious ritual…with their hands…broke a little piece of bread from the loaf and dunked it into the wine, and ate it. It was good. It warmed them, inside and out.

Tony loved the bread he would get in Italy and some of the old bakeries in Utica, and now…since that trip… Spanish bread was on the same desirable list.

Tony…but maybe not his wife… knew in his heart of hearts…he knew, then and there… he would never forget this day. How could he???

The sun broke through what was, a few minutes ago, a thick lid of gray clouds.

They found a seat in the circular bullfighting arena and with her usual foresight; his wife miraculously produced two plastic grocery size bags from her purse. The stone bleacher seats were still a little wet from the all day rain. Thank God, it had stopped raining.

And the bulls…five of them in all…the magnificent bulls…came charging out one at a time into the center of the arena…most still had the picador's spears stuck in their jet black, long and powerful shiny necks…angry…snorting…alternately pounding one, then the other, of their front hoofs into the sandy soil. *His neck and his head are enormous…I never realized both were so big…that big!!! Wow!!! It is more than half of his whole body…sure as shit… more than half his weight...look at him turn…and twist and pivot…he probably can turn on a dime...he's so agile...he is so big...so defiant... so strong... so invincible.*

But, he's going to die and he is to going to die today…as are the four others who will follow him…and the schools and the hospitals in the surrounding mountain villages (according to what Tony was told) will eat the flesh of their bodies. The school children will be nourished and satisfied and made to grow strong. The infirm, the sick and the lame will also partake and they too will gain strength and live.

The matador and the bull always…as they have since time immemorial…preformed admirably. Occasionally, a horse mounted picador would ride out and jab and stick the bull with his spear. They say it is to keep him angry, to make a fight of it, but in reality it is to sap yet more strength from this magnificent beast and weaken him.

The beast's eyes always sought out the matador and…he…the matador…with his silky colorful cape…continued to taunt and aggravate the bull. The animal soon showed signs of weakening; his pelt became shinier as blood mixed with his sweat. A large blood stain appeared on the Toro's left shoulder, and for some unknown reason, Tony felt the shiny red and black stain made the animal appear larger and more potent. Dangerous.

The stains were most prominent about the wounds the picador had inflicted in that tremendous neck. The sweat and the stains would flash and flicker and reflect and reveal…in a fraction of a microsecond…a silver streak which instantly disappeared in the now bright Spanish sunlight.

The bull had been totally sapped of his magnificent agility and strength. The end was near and you felt he too welcomed the forthcoming eternal rest...he didn't lunge or pivot anymore. He kept lowering his head…eyes on the matador…still punishing the arena floor with one or the other of his hoofs…and appeared to struggle just to raise his head higher, one more time. He nonetheless did so, because something forced him to face and destroy the taunting, dancing, silk cape. He was, by this time, breathing and panting like no other animal Tony had ever seen. The end was very near.

The matador in his suit of lights was tired too and was ready to perform his final act. The bull raised his head to its full and highest natural height, loudly groaned and howled and roared and screamed…the desperate and mournful sounds rippled up into the arena and surrounded the crowd…Tony's wife gasped, closed her eyes tightly and looked away. That brave bull slowly lowered his enormous head; his snout almost touching the arena sandy soil…the moment of truth….the matador mercifully inserted his saber into the animal's forehead. The beast first fell on his rear haunches, tried to howl again…but it was not as loud…and collapsed into the slightly damp… almost dry soil of the arena.

The matador strutted out of the arena. Soon after, two men leading a team of oxen came to the bull. One of the men started to place a harness about the fallen animal's neck, and the other drew out a dagger or knife, went to his neck, and very quickly and professionally, cut the jugular vein. The animal's remaining blood soon left his body and was absorbed into the arena soil.

Tony…but maybe not his wife…knew…he just knew from the deepest crevices of his heart…he knew, then and there…he would never forget this day. How could he???

He never regretted it either. He often thought and reflected (if that is the correct word) on how much like animals we are and how much superior (if that is the correct word) we are to animals.

Pg Up

The neighborhood was going downhill, and going fast. The landlords (*le patrone*) of the brownstones and the three deckers where having trouble finding renters. Slowly, like a creeping and painful cancer snaking its way to an inevitable demise, the 'owners' abandoned many to the tax rolls and others sold them off for just pennies on the dollar…if they could. They were sapped of their patience and just gave up trying. The N.D. Peters Construction Company really tried to save their buildings, but it was like the guys used to say, "you ain't gunna stay dry trying to piss wid da wind blowin in your face."

No doubt, one or two became crack houses or housing for the homeless and derelicts. The noble and honored Melchiorre house did not escape this fate. In time, there was a fire in one of the second floor rear apartments…the one on the right. The fire was contained, but burned rapidly, charring the outside wall in that corner up as far as the roofline.

An ugly, black blotch that could easily been seen from the Brandegee School playground which, ironically enough, was being closed next year because of budgetary difficulties. Such an ugly black scar upon an old, and once very magnificent and noble gray lady.

It was condemned. They stripped her veins and arteries…her wires and lead plumbing… and carted them off. Soon children would be playing and scavenging in the debris and the rubble of broken, twisted, shattered boards. Sometimes the kids would find a treasure, some small token of the lives that had been lived in that house, so long ago.

They filled the basement with some of the debris and mounded it…a good four feet from the original street line…allowing for natural settlement.

The kids…all of which are God's children…played on the mound and continued to do so until the mound did indeed settle. When some of the kids bent over, it reminded Tony of bent, barren corn stalks creased half way up from the bottom…in the center… (*Steinbeck could tell ya how dey looked...like he wrote about in the Grapes of Wrath and dose merciless dust storms)* bent…but not broken…and at a right angle to the rubbish beneath their feet. Eventually, it was covered with inexpensive creek shale. Weeds grew here and there.

And some of the old timers in the neighborhood swear they can still hear the rumbling of the trucks and screech of the whistles from the mills and some even say…they can hear the sad soft groans…and distant screams and mournful moans coming from underneath the buried debris at the Melchiorre house. Some say that it is the sound of a mother weeping for lost sons…*but still...it is better here than it was in the old country.*

Of course…that is only if you truly believe the Melchiorre House to be a LADY who possessed all the motherly instinct that accompany child-bearing and child-raising.

Hat Box Becky

Pg Up

Hat Box Becky was a prostitute. She was sort of the senior member of a 'stable' that worked out of Union City, New Jersey and was, like the other working girls in the stable, the property of a well established family engaging in various illegal activities including this: the oldest profession known to man. During Prohibition, this particular family made and maintained arrangements with other quasi-organized associates. Roughly it branched out from New York City and northeastern New Jersey, up the Hudson to Albany, crossing and forming the 'T': Buffalo-Albany-Boston. The 'T' had northerly spurs to Montréal (out of Albany) and from Utica to Massena and Watertown. The King, English Parliament and Canada did not sense or feel the moral obligation to prohibit the consumption of alcohol, nor did they wish to participate in the Noble Experiment. The Noble Experiment (Prohibition) glowed brightly…burst…burned fast and furious…and as quickly as it came upon the public, it disappeared and was forgotten. Not so…not so...with the oldest profession known to mankind…not so.

The 'T Circuit' was used by twelve groups of four working girls and was rotated monthly. They serviced eleven houses (brothels/cat houses) on the circuit. Then, after a full eleven-month cycle of work, they earned an all expenses paid vacation for the twelfth month. The working girls, regardless of what many assume to be a special feature of their profession, were far from just having fun and getting carnal satisfaction. They would want and need a periodic change of venue from that type of lifestyle…and above all…they needed rest.

Becky and her girls traveled by train. They used a large steamer trunk for all their clothing. Some people, but again not all, thought them to be showgirls…a flashback on the old vaudeville days. In addition to the large brass plated and leather belts that secured the steamer trunk, (which had ample room for all the girls' clothing) Becky always hand carried a blue and green hat box when traveling. Picture hats were very popular, especially in those days...

Becky was a tall, shapely woman with equally shapely long legs, and long reddish brown hair. You just knew…just by looking at her…that she must have at one time aspired to be a dancer and or a showgirl. She looked outstanding when wearing a picture hat. She could turn heads…both female and male…whenever she wore it. She was graceful in her gait and the guys would say, "she must be a dancer, or should have been one."

Hat Box Becky had only two picture hats, one she was wearing, and the other was carefully stored in the steamer trunk. In her blue and green hatbox, she carried and stored a lamp and a lampshade. The lampshade was always pink, (she had replaced several over the years) and the lamp itself was made of ceramic and had red and black on/off buttons... You would push the red button and the black button would disappear into the mechanism and vise versa.

The lamp itself had a five inch circular red base, resembling a Broadway stage and rising platform, that acted as support for perfectly shaped dancer's legs…in spiked black, shiny high heels and the right knee slightly pinching-overlapping the left knee. At the top, just below the brass lamp mechanism, was depicted a blue fluffy crinoline tutu. No other body parts were shown. The shape of the legs was perfect, just as Becky's were…well at one time anyway! Whenever she arrived for a monthly tour, she would set up the lamp, with its pink lampshade, upon the nightstand by the bed. It was special to her, but the story behind it is much too sad to tell.

…and…there was…

Johnny, "the Hammer" who was a midget/dwarf. His father was ashamed of him because of his size, which only caused his mother to love him even more. The Hammer left home well before he was sixteen: he left home but not Utica. Those early years of bickering and arguing (and occasional one sided beatings he had endured at his father's hands) toughened him up in way that offset his lack of height.

The Hammer eventually became a doorman at the local cathouse. He started working for Ma Wilson, first in the kitchen (she furnished him a bed…an old baby crib), which was located in the large pantry right off of the kitchen. In time, he became invaluable to her and the operation, so much so that she'd spend most of the evenings sipping her expensive bourbon (always neat) and chatting with prominent clientele. She left the business end of it to Hammer. The transient employees/working girls became his charge…his GIRLS…and he protected them as his father should have protected him. The girls knew that and…because of it…loved him as much as Hammer's mother loved him.

Johnny the Hammer earned his nickname in a memorable manner. The talk on the street and at the taprooms and at the corner candy stores and coffee shops was accurate: *you don't fuck around with Johnny the Hammer.* It could easily remind you of an old Texas saying…"It isn't the size of the dog in a fight…it is the size of the fight in the dog."

The story goes a couple of years back, a loud mouth big...very big…lumberjack stopped at Ma Wilson's establishment seeking carnal satisfaction. The Hammer opened the front door for him and led him to the waiting parlor…"it won't be a long wait…just a couple of minutes." That was not a big problem for anyone. When one of the girls was free upstairs, the Hammer led him to the bedroom, the second room on the left. Michele's room. The Hammer introduced him to her and in his manner waddled down the stairs to take up his post at the locked front door. It didn't seem too long afterwards that a ruckus broke out upstairs…the second room to the left…the Hammer ran up the stairs as fast as his very short legs would carry him.

The big lumberjack was arguing about the cost. "Hey Fella you know the rules and the cost…nobody is trying to beat you out of a couple of bucks…you want something extra…ya gotta pay…you know that!!!"

The big lumberjack…who was half French and half native American and who had had maybe one or two stiff drinks before going to Ma Wilson, responded to the Hammer's plea for reasonableness in not too kindly a manner: he reached down, grabbed the Hammer by his left shoulder, spun him violently, reached down again and grabbed the Hammer's belt, secured his grip on the Hammer's collar and flung him down the stairs. When he got to the bottom, the Hammer was stunned and amazed. Pandemonium broke out upstairs.

The other three bedrooms emptied of clients and the working girls, all entering the hallway: the girls screaming, the men wide-eyed…like trapped animals looking for a way to escape. The male clients hopping and trying to put on their shoes, some trying to get back into their trousers…the girls wrapping and pulling their silky robes around not too heavily clad bodies. The tall lumberjack was now laughing…roaring…at the plight and dilemma of those less fortunate than he...as he stood in the center of the hallway.

The Hammer got to his feet…nothing and everything was hurting…yet…he knew he had to get upstairs…he was needed. He charged up the stairs again, avoiding those scrambling down. The lumberjack watched the fleeing…roaring…and making catcalls. Up came the dwarf/midget…up those 14 steps…to his Goliath. When he reached the tenth step, the giant yelled…"ehe…my little half man…you want more??? Throwing you down the stairs was not enough??? Ehe??? Try this!!!"

The big man kicked him. The toe of his boot caught the tough little doorman squarely at his mouth. As he fell backwards and down those steps, he tasted the salt of his blood in his mouth, when he reached the landing he rolled over on his right side and instinctively spat out four of his small front teeth, two still clung loosely to his gums, like broken branches that did not snap clean. Now it hurt. His head was spinning, he tried to shake it clear, and he tried to focus up there…up there...at the top of the flight of stairs. Just a blur, he shook his head again…his face hurt. He knew he was needed upstairs.

The dwarf, scrambled to his feet, he fell. He got up on all fours and reached for the stair railing and straightened up and stood. Still wobbly, very wobbly and hurting…hurting…*my head...my head* he stumbled into the kitchen and in the cupboard beneath the sink, wrapped in a towel he found what he was looking for. The brave little man again went to the staircase and started his arduous journey to the top. He was needed…one of his girls needed help. The waiting room had cleared out, and police sirens could be heard coming in the direction of the establishment.

With a mouth full of blood and pain, he climbed the steps and found the drunken lumberjack going through the prostitute Michele's purse. She had fainted and lay in the doorway to her room. With a fist full of five dollar bills, the lumber jack stepped over the unconscious girl and headed for the staircase, and as he did so, he came face to face with the little, bloody dwarf. He saw that he had a snub nose 38-caliber pistol in his small…but very steady hand.

The dwarf was aiming at his groin. The lumberjack saw this but even before he saw the aim, he sensed it and immediately lunged to the right seeking the safety of the prostitute's bedroom. The blast of the gunshot echoed in the upstairs hallway, shattered the silence of the once crowded waiting room, spread to the street and reached the ears of the policemen as they came storming out of their patrol cars. Two had arrived simultaneously; the third could be heard screaming down Catherine Street.

The bullet shattered and almost severed the femur bone in the lumberjack's left thigh. When the police arrived upon the scene, they found three unconscious people: a drunken lumberjack, a young and frightened prostitute and someone who was not quite four feet in height, but as brave and courageous a man as you'd ever want to know.

What happened afterwards is really how the midget doorman got his nickname.

The newspapers reported the story as a intoxicated guest at a hotel was found in the act of stealing money from a hotel worker, attempted to flee, and was shot in the thigh. The guest, supposedly a Canadian citizen, is scheduled to stand a hearing on such and such a day, pending early release from Memorial Hospital. The lumber company posted his bail and the court granted him freedom on his own recognizance. The police were not obligated to post a guard at the hospital.

About five days after the shooting, the doorman visited the lumberjack in the hospital. He gave him a carton of Camel cigarettes, which he carried in a grocery bag. He also had carried a ball-peen hammer in the same bag. The lumberjack was in a ten bed male ward on the second floor, and there were only five beds occupied. The hospitalized Canadian who spoke more French than English, said *Merci*, when the dwarf gave him the carton and genuinely smiled at him. Hammer just nodded in recognition.

The Hammer reached down by the foot of the hospital bed, and picked up the small wooden (newly painted white) stepstool used to help patients get in out of the bed. It was designed so that in the center of the step platform was a carved out hole resembling a plump bratwurst; the opening was a convenient and a clever four finger-carrying handle. The Hammer brought it up to the head of the bed, carefully stepped upon the platform, reached into the paper bag and pulled out the ball-peen hammer.

He struck the lumberjack squarely in the mouth, making sure that the hammer made contact with the flat side (greater area) and not the head. Blood splattered onto the white sheets and even the midget's right sleeve. He spat at the once again wounded lumberjack and hissed, "I should kill you!!! You lousy son of a bitch!!!"

At the hearing, the judge noted that the Canadian citizen also suffered a 'falling accident' while in the hospital. The five other male patients in the ward were all asleep when the accident occurred and didn't know or see anything. A giant of a man left Utica and New York State and the United States, on crutches and missing four front teeth.

The afternoon following the date of the falling accident, Hammer visited his Mom. "Nannee Nunnee (was how she would say Johnny or try to say John) how you be...whadda happen to you mouthda???...youda get hurt ??? youda all rigtha???"

Hammer visited his mother at least twice a month, making sure she was okay and didn't need anything. He did this even more so, now that his younger sister married and moved to small apartment, way over on the west side. He always made sure his father wasn't home when he visited. Two months ago, Hammer bought her a Westinghouse refrigerator. It had a small ice compartment with two trays to make ice cubes. What a wonderful and beautiful thing it was to her. She could make her own ice, all summer long she would polish and buff the white enamel finished appliance every day. In the upper right hand portion of the door was the Westinghouse logo, a small green circle...which looked like it had a comet tail coming out from the center...straight like an arrow...and telling you

Westinghouse…she marveled at this appliance. And even more so at the lettering and the strange letters in the American alphabet…like H and W.

"E niente Ma…niente…(It is nothing ma nothing)…you need anything Ma…???"
She always answered the same, but the Hammer would leave a couple of twenties every time he visited..."I gotta nuff…you putta in da banka…I gotta enuffa!" He'd leave it anyway.

"The bank doesn't need it Ma…you use it…you let me know if you need anything…anything Ma!!!…Okay???"

The Hammer was a good, caring and loving son. However, the talk on the street, in the taprooms, at the corner candy stores and the coffee shops was to remain unchanged; *you don't fuck around with the Hammer.*

The stable was changing at Ma Wilson's house. "Hammer, the girls are coming in on the 3:45." He knew and, he knew it was Hat Box Betty's crew. Good kids, Hammer liked them, he always did. It was a great day in the merry month of May, not a cloud in the sky and a warmth that told you summer was coming. The Hammer just bought a Buick convertible, yellow…and with four small circular holes on both sides on the hood....*yeah in England they call it the Bonnet...imagine that!!!* The vehicle…like all those that The Hammer drove…was modified so that the shifting of gears, the acceleration and braking was all done from the steering wheel.

The New York Central 3:45 was on time. Two Red Caps struggled with the large steamer trunk, placing it on a four-wheeled gurney; and then side-by-side started pushing the gurney. The two black Red Caps, beaming with pride and happiness, led and escorted a procession of four young, beautifully dressed girls (one of which had a wide and handsome picture hat) and a waddling midget from the baggage area through the large Union Station waiting room and ticket area, to one of the Broad Street exits…under those enormous wooden awnings that circled Union station…right up to Mr. Hammer's shiny new…*aut toe mo beal*…(parked in front of a fire hydrant). They struggle to put the steamer in the Buick: as big as the automobile trunk was, they still had to tie down the back lid with some twine….*yeah…in England they call it a hood…imagine that!!!*

The Hammer reached into his pocket, pulled out his money clip, peeled two fives and gave one each to the Red Caps. In unison, they said, "WHY Thank You Mr. Hammer…Thank you very much." They then touched the black shiny brim of their hats and said, "Have a good day ladies…enjoy your stay…" Side by side they both pushed the gurney back to the baggage section, smiling broadly and bobbing their heads.

The new yellow Buick, with its roof retracted, was parked by the hydrant and looked very inviting and handsome. One of the girls half giggled half whispered, "this is beautiful just like Cinderella's pumpkin carriage." Hat Box Becky and Johnny the Hammer opened their doors to allow the three girls to get into the backseat…"What a beautiful car this is Hammer…good luck with it!!! I just love the color!!!" The three working girls, wobbly in their high heels, stepped into the rear seat and patted and felt the softness of the leather seats. "I feel like a Princess!!!"

"All four of you **are**!" said The Hammer, and the working girls felt very special: Johnny the Hammer could make you feel like somebody so easily. "We gotta lotta time…you ladies wanna go for a ride???" They'd love to, of course!!! This little ritual became a precedent…weather permitting, whenever there was a stable change. Becky got in the passenger side, shut the car door and placed her hatbox squarely on her lap and smiled as broadly as any one of the other girls.

The Hammer drove up to Bagg's Square, got onto the main drag, Genesee Street and traveled south-westerly (almost the entire length of Genesee Street) to the Parkway. Should he see someone he knew…or thought he knew…he would toot his horn. An open convertible with a dwarf driver and four shapely, smiling and laughing girls in it really did not have to be tooted to be noticed. If someone recognized The Hammer they would wave, and the younger girls in the back would gladly and willingly return a greeting. They loved it, all four of them were princesses and they were riding in a Golden Pumpkin.

At the Parkway, they turned left, passed the wealthy doctors and lawyers and Indian chief's homes, and continued on to pass the South Woods Park (the Eagle) and Roscoe Conkling Park. When the Golden Pumpkin arrived at the intersection of the Parkway and Mohawk Street, it turned left and headed north. They drove all the way down Mohawk Street, to Bleecker, and there, at the intersection waiting for the street light to change, The Hammer tooted the horn again, told the girls to look to the left and wave to the guys hanging around the Mello Shop.

The one car cortege turned right onto Bleecker and headed east. Within three or four city blocks they were parading by The Goody Shop Luncheonette. The Hammer tooted the horn at the Goody Shop guys hanging around in front by the news rack and the girls in the back seat with welcoming enthusiasm all smiled in their direction. Catcalls came from the Goody Shop guys, "Hey Hammer, got a new batch?" And, "Hey Hammer ya takin all those girls to Hollywood for a screen test?"

The big Buick turned left onto Kossuth Avenue, it only had to travel about three blocks to get to Catherine Street. Becky looked straight ahead, all the way down to Broad Street. Kossuth ended at Broad, and the scene she saw, was of course, the tenement houses…some two story frame houses…on right and left…but what dominated it all to her was the five story textile mill. It seemed like it was a wall that kept prisoners in…a deterrent…something between you and an open field and freedom. She shook her head and let the melancholy thought go.

The Hammer turned left onto Catherine Street, the last leg of their Pumpkin ride. At mid-block, and in front of the Melchiorre house and Brandegee Schoolyard, was N.D. Peter's Cement yard. The work crews and cement truck drivers had returned from the various job sites and deliveries; it was quitting time and time to go home. They all exited the Catherine Street gate. Perfect timing!!!

As they were leaving the construction yard, the big Golden Pumpkin was right there cruising by the front gate. The Hammer did not have to blow the horn; instead he came to a complete stop right there in the middle of the street. Then, many of the workmen put their metal lunch pails on the ground and applauded vigorously calling out in jovial and welcoming tones. One of the girls seated in the rear stood up, put her arms straight out, wiggled her hips and shoulders simultaneously…bouncing an abundantly endowed bosom…and smiled broadly. The other girls also waved and sung out greetings, even Becky half smiled: she had quite forgotten the gray feeling she experienced when she saw the walls of the textile mill.

The shouting and the catcalls became overwhelming. Everybody was smiling and happy, many of the witnesses and participants carried that memory to their grave. The Hammer put the vehicle in gear and slowly continued down Catherine Street. Slowly gliding by the Melchiorre House, only he and Becky heard and saw a little girl jumping rope and singing…"Hitler is a Jerk…Mussolini is a weenie...but the Japs are worse."

A few yards down the street, as the Golden Pumpkin passed the schoolyard, Tony and Buster and Jack and Pat and Frankie and all the other guys were playing a game of softball. They all stopped in their tracks so to say;

to watch the Buick, now accelerating slightly, move on by. The boys all noticed and gawked at the passengers and watched as the vehicle disappeared down the street. Tony noticed the steamer trunk protruding out of the Buick's trunk and it reminded him of his Uncle Joe and Zia Grazia. *They had one just like dat one...*

When the Golden Pumpkin arrived at Ma Wilson's, the girls scrambled into the kitchen cackling like happy hens, or school girls going out to recess, said their greetings and were all treated to a cool glass of lemonade. The Hammer found Harry the Mayor (an alcoholic) who was always around and pressed him into service. Struggling, they took the steamer trunk from the Buick and climbed the front staircase. Harry pissed and moaned all the way up, even though he led and The Hammer's small compact body took the brunt of the weight and the awkwardness of the luggage, his red face pressing against the side hand grip...his hands lifting and pushing on the bottom. Finally, they made it. The trunk was placed in Becky's room; it was the largest of the four rooms on the second floor.

Later that afternoon, Becky, carrying her famous hat box, went to her room, removed the small lamp that Ma Wilson had provided, carefully placed her lamp on the dresser that had a circular mirror over it, and attached the pink lamp shade. She stepped back and once again, half smiled as she studied her leggy statue. She put Ma Wilson's lamp on the floor in the rear of the hall closet for safekeeping.

She returned to the room, and this time with a full smile on her pretty face, she admired the leggy statuette. She really didn't know why, but that little lamp always made her feel good...like Johnny The Hammer...it made her feel like something special, a somebody. She gently touched the blue tutu, and then ran her finger slowly down the dancer's leg.

She was genuinely smiling when she stood in that little room and she not only felt radiant, but also ***was*** radiant and glowing. Still smiling, she touched the blue-fluffed crinoline tutu again. That little lamp always made her feel special…like Johnny Hammer …and other nice people who treated her kind of *special.*

Then, she went to the steamer trunk, found her neatly folded blue and gold kimono (the other girls had taken out their belongings earlier), got clean underwear and bra, found a towel and took a shower. *Post time ladies and gentlemen...post time* …in another three quarters of an hour… she and her stable mates will be working.

They did indeed…all of them…work hard for their money.

Whooze Gonna Tell da Story

Pg Dn

Nunzio had a file. Really just some papers…letters…telegrams…newspaper clippings…and a wallet size photograph of a smiling soldier, of his brother Joey. Nunzio gave Tony photocopies of everything except the photo.

Tony remembered his 'let's have a drink' meetings with Nunzio at the VFW 4321 and another meeting once at Marr-Logg's for breakfast. He remembered bits and flashes of the dialogue, the tones, the variance of the pitches, the brow knitting, facial expressions all showing the feelings and the mood of what was being recounted, and some of it was even said aloud. But not all.

He remembered them all so clearly that they continued to haunt him somehow or another. (Tony always thought that *haunt* was a strong word…descriptive…a depressing word…mysterious, bordering on the supernatural…conjuring up dark sad memories.) Sort of like the blurred memories of a partially recalled bad dream…those dreams you want to forget…but cannot. That gnawing sense when you are on the edge of something and you are losing control of your surroundings…you fear you are about to fall into its abyss…and you are frightened…frightened to find out the truth or what the truth may not be.

Tony has a very thick paperbound book on his desk (over 600 pages), a slew of computer generated copy sheets (twenty-three pages in all and neatly kept in a stack by an oversized paper clip), photocopies of two hand written letters (…in script…one dated 1950, the other 1953), a reduced copy of the front page of the Utica Observer Dispatch…dated June 25th, 1951…two copies of Western Union messages, and just one other small thing.

From an old shoe box filled with snapshots and studio pictures that was bequeathed to him after his mother's death, Tony had a very old and small snapshot of four teenaged couples. It had to be in June and…he was positive of the year and the month…taken in 1947. It was taken the night of the Senior Ball at Thomas R. Proctor High School. Eight smiling kids, the girls in gowns, all wearing a corsage: the boys in black and white rented tuxedos (some of them even had to rent black shoes) with bow ties, and a carnation in their white lapels.

And…there…over there on the far end...aside Carmine Bossone and Dorie Alito …is Joey Melchiorre… grinning back into the Kodak Brownie lens, waiting for the flash to go off. His nickname: Firpo.

Tony wanted to tell Joey's story…and he wanted to do it right…Joey and the Melchiorre family deserved nothing less than that. Tony struggled…and then he slept on it…and he struggled again…and then slept on it again.

And it came to him…like, it is said, *a bolt of lightening*, but as Tony prefers…out of a clear blue sky on a warm June morning. His conscience told him....*whatza dere to struggle about you big goof...let da printed and the hand written word tell the story....yur gunna talk yourself into dat and then dat and miss da whole point of the story...*

Pg Up

The Senior Ball was always held on a Saturday night. The guys would make arrangements as to whose car to borrow ("Didja try yur brother Cosmo…betcha Johnny Dee would let ya borrow his…") and, as a sort of covenant to the loan, the guys would clean and wash and wax the vehicle. Salvatore and Joey decided to ask Johnny Dee.

"When? This Saturday…oh Next week…sure ya can…maybe you can pick it up Saturday noon at Scampy's…I go to the track with Mike Tamer every

Saturday and we always go back to Scampy's…we'll probably be dare till closing…anyway Scamp always locks the doors after two…but we'll be inside….I can't go home until six in the morning anyway…My mother won't let me in anyway till after six…she'd think I was a stranger or something…" They all laughed and thought what a good guy Johnny was.

At exactly noon of the big day, Sal and Joey walked into Scampy's, and the taproom was jumping. Soon after Scampy purchased the bar from Big John Cappocio, and with the help of some political connections and 'favors' owed to his father, he installed a ticker tape machine. Shortly thereafter, a very large green slate 'blackboard' went up along the interior supporting wall dividing the bar from the restaurant area. The slate had yellow printing and various vertical and horizontal lines. On one half of the board…across the top and in bold uppercase lettering was: **AMERICAN LEAGUE**, on the other, **NATIONAL LEAGUE**.

The Western Electric ticker tape machine was installed between the phone booth and the 'Big Board' as it was to become known. The ticker tape was on a little pedestal four and half feet above the tap room floor and it had a test tube type glass bowl protecting its mechanisms. Scampy placed a tall circular Wheeling, West Virginia trash can beneath to catch and gather the ribbon of printed tape as it was being read. Specifically assigned personnel posted results. There was a small, four-step, wooden ladder used by the designated people to reach up and post the results, or lack of results, for each inning as the various games progressed. When there was a weekday game there was always activity. It was however, nothing compared to Saturdays and Sundays (in the summer) when Scampy's place was really jumping.

An illegal bet or two may have occurred during the course of the 'business day'.

"Hey Johnny!!!...let me buy youse guys a drink", was how Tony's brother greeted his Army Veteran cousin Johnny and his Navy Veteran buddy Mike. Both were there since before eleven watching and waiting for various betting lines to change. (*Good old Johnny...like a brick...solid...dependable...said he'd be here...and there he is...bet you his navy buddy Mike is da same...ya gotta love dem guys!)* In those days, you could drink and get drafted at eighteen, but had to be twenty-one to vote.

"Naw, Sally save yur money…you may need it for tonight," both John and Mike smiled at the younger boys and their obvious excitement about going to the big dance with fancy clothes and stuff like that. "Ears da car keys…me and Mike are goin to the track for the flats and maybe stay for the schully…see ya ear bout one, two in the morning…alright?"

"Yeah…sure! Tanks…we wanna take it now so we can wash and wax it…ya know?" John and Mike both smiled at the 'kids' and John bobbed his head giving them a physical sign of approval. "Ya sure youse don't want a drink or sumptin?" The army veteran of General Patton's Third Army and the Navy veteran of 28 months on a mine sweeper in the pacific, shook their heads no and they all said "see ya later" in unison.

The younger men left the bar and the older (the veterans) returned to watching and listening to what the lines were and occasionally sipping their beers and just talking. Their conversation some how drifted and lit upon Hiroshima and the A-Bomb.

"Ya know what I remembered bout that…is when we got the news…we were all leaving the movie auditorium in the hospital (they dug shrapnel out of Johnny's right thigh and attended to a facial wound…also on the right side…he was wounded in March, 1945)…we had just seen the movie picture *Arsenic and Old Lace* and some of the guys had crutches and as we was leavin the auditorium a couple of 'em would yell CHARGE and hold up one crutch…by the time we got to the bunks we was all doin it!!!"

And Mike, too, could pinpoint when and were he heard the news about Hiroshima. "I was standing 12 to 4 night watch on that tin bucket of nuts and bolts they called a mine sweeper…betcha the Japs' sub had us in dare sights a hundred times but decided it wasn't worth a good torpedo to blow it outda da water….anyway…they flashed the message from a nearby cruiser to us and a couple of destroyers nearby….I tell ya what John….I was as happy as a pig in shit on a Sunday morning who had just gotten laid to hear that news. To me, it meant the war was over and all we had to do was to keep that rusty bucket afloat and get it home eventually."

About a half hour later, Johnny and Mike said their good-byes and went to the racetrack. Sal and Joey met Carlo and Carmine at Proctor Park, to wash and wax the sedans they had borrowed for the evening. They all had their own family's zinc buckets (mostly used when the kids went bean picking in the summer months) and willingly shared sponges and rags and towels to complete the task. It turned out to be a beautiful, warm, cloudless afternoon.

"Ya know sumptin??? ya just can't beat the way a big four-door black car shines up…'specially at night when utter lights reflect off of it….maybe dey look like dey show more dirt dan utter colors but ya can't beat they way dey look when ya do a good job of waxin." They all agreed. They turned over the bean picking buckets, lit up two Lucky Strikes cigarettes, sat on the buckets and shared a smoke. They all faced the two shiny vehicles and admired the end result of their afternoon's labor, there in Proctor Park, by the creek.

Pg Dn

Tony picked up the office type folder which read "The Melchiorre Papers" written in red on the face. He carefully slipped the letter-sized envelope out from under a paper clip, fingered the envelope and then gently pulled out the old photo. Gently…like almost being frightened of it, he held it and studied it again. Happy…smiling…kids…God Bless America, land that I love.

Later…later…I'll think about it later…

He returned it. The paper clip that held the photo envelope also had other papers clipped to it. The one on top was a photocopy of the front page of the Utica Observer Dispatch dated July 26th. The third paragraph of an item in the fifth column, directly beneath the center fold reads: **Melchiorre volunteered for service August 9, 1948 for a three–year term. He went overseas in December and had been with the 21st Infantry in Japan.**

Pg Up

Joey and Dorie. Dorie Alito, one of the six Alito girls…she was number three…and of all those kids she had only one brother, who was the second to last child of their clan. Joey and Dorie were going 'steady' ever since that Christmas party at St. Anthony's basement/auditorium/religious instruction classroom/sometime dinner-dance location/rec-hall. And Joey was nuts about her, he felt like it was for all of his life, but it wasn't. Starting two summers ago on a bright sunny Sunday morning, Joey noticed how pretty Dorie was when he caught a glimpse of her walking with a stout, saintly mother and five sisters who seemed to be in lock step…all marching…two by two up…all spanky clean and shiny and angelic. They were going to Mass.

Julia, her mother whom everyone loved, would lead the procession with her youngest clinging to her left hand and swinging her small black imitation leather purse casually and graceful in her right hand, the two eldest girls brought up the rear. The Alito ladies walked up Kossuth and then turned right onto Bleecker Street. They belonged to St. Anthony's Parish…*la parrocchia di Santo Antonio* the old timers used to say.

Their brother Pasquale (who wanted to be called Pat by his friends and all those he could beat up…and really not having a say in what the adults in his family called him) would go to the eleven-thirty Mass with his father.

The Melchiorre family lived on the west side of Kossuth and went to Our Lady of Mount Carmel; Father Pizzoglio's parrocchia. And Joey was nuts about Dorie.

On Sunday mornings, (even in the wintertime…Joey in a hand-me-down army field jacket would stand by Marraffa's Fish Market and watch "his girl"…the most beautiful of all…walk up the opposite side of the street. He would follow at a safe distance till he came up to Joe the Barber's and sometimes even as far as Scampy's place…but always on the Mt. Carmel side of Kossuth.

Of late, Joey could not wait until after Sunday dinner….til two o'clock…to go down the alleyway and up the rear staircase and knock on the Alito's kitchen door…take off and hold his hat with both hands when Mr. Altio answered…clear his throat…it seemed so raspy to him. Joey would stutter a greeting and something about if Dorie was home.

"Dorie…what does this kid want???" Mr. Alito knew, and whether he wanted to or not…he knew he had to be as stern and as dictatorial as possible…my God the guy had six girls…and these guys kept coming over interrupting his quiet Sunday afternoon...the Yanks were at home for a double header.

"You know, Daddy. I told you yesterday and this morning, that Joey and I wanted to go to the movies at the Stanley…the three o'clock matinee…I told you and Mommy."

Of course Mr. Alito knew, he had six girls and he knew everything. He came to America with six brothers and two sisters when he was all of three years old. He went to school up until he was fifteen, lied about his age and joined the Army in 1917. He was assigned to the fledgling Army Air Corps and eventually became a full fledged mechanic. When he got out, he went to work for one of the first Ford dealerships of Utica. He was a valued and trusted employee and was now in charge of the service department and garage. Mr. Alito knew everything.

The kids went to the movies that Sunday afternoon. They boarded the bus (the trolleys were replaced in 1946) at the corner of Kossuth and Bleecker Streets…twelve cents and a transfer each…and held hands on the bus and in the theater. They retraced the routine on the way home. Mr. Alito knew everything, and he knew that in two weeks the kids would be going to their high school senior ball and he knew Salvatore (Pete the Bariesse's oldest son) was borrowing Johnny Dee's black, shiny four-door Pontiac and he knew his daughter was going to wear one of her older sister's gown. His wife made some minor adjustments on the gown; which incidentally the older sister wore when she was in a wedding party back in April, the first Saturday after Easter.

Mr. Alito knew everything.

The day of the senior ball finally arrived. Sal and Joey in their rented tuxedos (with shoes $4.00, w/out $3.50) and corsages in square boxes with fancy ribbons around them, went to pick up their dates in a black shiny…just waxed…four-door Pontiac. They picked up Dorie first (Joey and Dorie were going steady you know!).

They both went upstairs via the back steps at the end of the alley. Julia Alito offered them a cold glass of lemonade. Upon leaving, Julia told the kids to be careful and have a good time… "Where are you going after the dance…oh, Trinkaus Manor…that's nice…be careful…" Mr. Alito just grunted, caught Salvatore's eye and then Joey's and ordered, "Don't be home too late."

Joey opened the left rear door of the Pontiac for Dorie…Sal and Joey deliberately parked on the wrong side of the street…so as to not let Dorie cross the street in her beautiful gown. Julia witnessed this from the front window of their apartment. She smiled and was very pleased that Joey was a real gentleman that opened and held the door for her Dorie. She returned to the kitchen and Mr. Alito was sitting at the kitchen table sipping on a glass of beer and Julia told him what a nice boy that Joey is…and a good family too!!!

Mr. Alito, who knew everything, just made an audible sound of recognition and said aloud, "Little Dorie looked so pretty," looked at the kitchen clock above the sink, then back to the sports page. He thought to himself…*Hail Mary Full of Grace…the Yanks are still in second place…only a half game out* and then turned to look at the box score of yesterday's game. His thoughts again returned to his Little Dorie…*boy she is cute…she reminds me of her mother when I first met her…*

The kids had a good…no a great…time. They danced…joked…laughed…teased one another…told stories…took photos…ate red meat and mixed vegetables and salads with five or six different forks and spoons and knives. They all had a great time.

After dinner Salvatore drove up to the Eagle, a hilltop lover's lane overlooking the city. The city lights spread out beneath them and, from up high, it all looked so romantic. The kids recognized the automobiles of other prom couples parked nearby. "Sal, don't do that…sit on your hands if you wanna kiss me…don't spoil the evening…"

Dorie giggled a little bit and Joey was embarrassed by his friend's aggressive behavior because…*What da hell??? Dorie was sitting right here too!!!*…and he was going to marry Dorie someday.

It was getting late…for the girls anyway…so they left lover's lane with its view of the city and took the girls home. Sal dropped off Dorie and Joey first. Joey said, "Hey Sal, you take Babe home and I'll meet you at Scampy's in a little bit…" it was just a block and half up Kossuth Avenue.

Joey and Dorie held hands as they walked up the alleyway, which was well lit by the outside porch light. Mr. Alito saw to it that the back porch light was on; it had been burning since nine o'clock. As they kissed goodnight at the bottom of the covered staircase the kitchen door opened, but no one appeared. They knew it was open and knew what it meant because…Mr. Alito knew everything, he had six daughters.

Joey walked the short distance to Scampy's and Johnny Dee and Mike were already there. Mike won big at the track and Johnny Dee broke even (well that is what he'd tell you). Both of them had parlayed the Yankees and Red Sox and Indians games, and scored big. The World War II veterans were in a very good mood. They saw a smiling and happy Joey walk in and stepped away from the bar mockingly applauding at Joey's entrance, still looking dapper in his rented tuxedo. "Hey, make way for da lovely and talented Cary Grant, will ya?"

"Have a drink lover boy…where is the other one?"

"He's comin…he'll be right here…told me to meet him here."

Tony's brother Sal appeared and was subject to the same verbal abuse and the drink offer. They made room for him to stand along side them at the bar. They talked a little about the track and the dance and the baseball scores.

Because he was flush with the bookie's money, Johnny Dee said to Mike, "Let's treat these two movie stars to the cat house. Maybe with four of us we can get a discount." No one openly objected.

Although it would be the first time for Joey and he was a little frightened (Sal had been there before) Joey did not want to lose face, nor could he plead poverty, it was the bookie's money. Mike the 'old' minesweeper sailor said to Johnny Dee, "Let's me and you ride in the back seat and tell the whores and Johnny Hammer these two clowns in tuxedos are our chauffer and personal doorman."

Sal drove the black shiny Pontiac, which was good. The older boys may have had a little too much to drink anyway. The working girls didn't like it too much when guys came for their professional services and maybe had too much to drink. It forced them to work harder. *You didn't have too much to drink...did ya honey???*

The dwarf, Hammer, opened the front door at Ma Wilson's hotel for the foursome (two in tuxedos) and led them into the front parlor. The parlor was crowded. It was, of course, Saturday night or early Sunday morning. All the joints would soon start closing and, believe it or not, there was a full moon. Ma Wilson's stable of working girls were gunna be working hard tonight…very hard.

The Hammer came into the parlor and announced, "Two of the girls are ready…which two guys will it be?"…a momentary pause…and with a smile and a slight jerk of his head Johnny Dee motioned to the tuxedo clad youths. "Okay youse two guys, follow me."

Up the stairs they went, the midget first, Sal next (he was anxious) and then Joey, who was half frightened and half anxious and not all too sure he wanted to do this. At the top of the landing, two girls wearing colorful kimonos and high heels where standing in the doorways of their individual bedrooms. The Hammer said, "Hat Box you take the short one," turned and half waddled, half ran down the staircase. His position and post was by the front door and he wasn't sure he had properly locked it before he took the kids in the tuxedos upstairs. He checked the waiting parlor first (no new faces) and then went to make sure the door was locked. It was. *This is gunna be a busy night,* he thought.

Becky looked at Joey as he entered her room and smiled to herself in a motherly kind of way; she had a hunch this kid was a first timer. And she almost whispered to him… *It'll be alright kid,* she didn't want the kid to be afraid of the unknown.

With a simple hand gesture which the wide-eyed client followed with his eyes, she showed him where the clothes tree was. It took a moment, but then Joey understood. He undressed, just leaving his black socks on…the socks were not really his either, they belonged to his older brother Danny. He quietly watched Becky as she approached him with a small basin of warm soapy water, a bar of Ivory soap floating in it, and a blue towel hanging from her forearm like a waiter in a fancy restaurant.

It was house procedure, nobody wanted any a part of VD. She washed and examined him and was satisfied. *He was a first timer!!!* Joey lay on the queen size bed, at first staring only at the ceiling, then he turned his head to the left and noticed a lamp that had showgirl legs, with one knee sort of crossing over the other.

He closed his eyes for a minute or two, as Becky started to reveal to him what the unknown was all about. Suddenly, his eyes popped wide open…he could not close them if he wanted to...his lower abdomen erupted, his back arched, shoulders and heels pressing into the mattress. And then, it was over. He sighed and quietly looked at the dresser lamp with the shapely legs of a dancer with a blue tutu.

Joey now knew just a little bit more of life and some of the unknown.

Utica Observer-Dispatch

Melchiorre volunteered for service Aug. 9, 1948 for a three year term. He went overseas in December and had been with the 21st Infantry Regiment.

Where Blood was Shed

Pg Up

It was the Memorial Day weekend, in late May (of course) and Ant-Knee called Tony from Utica, in what was one of many such not too welcome calls. Young Ant-knee seemed to have somehow inherited an unwanted duty…he had to make "those" calls. He had some bad news.

Tony's first cousin and Ant-knee's baptismal Godfather, Johnny Dee, was struck by a vehicle on Albany Street, near Elizabeth Street, and was rushed to Saint E's emergency room. The story was, he had gone to Pescatore's Pizzeria to get pizza for his mother and one of his younger sisters, who was visiting from Syracuse. It was well after dark and it was raining, just slightly. Pescatore's was only a block and half away and in spite of the weather, Johnny Dee decided to walk. It was too much of a hassle; opening the swinging garage doors at the end of the long driveway, getting in and out of the car, finding a parking space, and then reversing the routine.

"It's only around the corner…it ain't raining that hard…I'll wear a hat and my light windbreaker…go ahead call in the order…everything on the pizza except onions…anchovies on the side…get the large…and…get an idea of how long it'll be…let me know how long…" Still a good old sergeant, making a plan and advising and mobilizing.

He left the house about five minutes earlier than needed; he could always talk to the Pesky brothers about the daily double at Vernon Downs. "Hey Johnny did ja bet dat tree legged horse???" Or, "How did Ring-eye-Pete do in the fort???" Later, he dutifully picked up the pizza in the large white cardboard carton, paid for it, said his good-byes to the Pesky brothers and left.

Nick went back into the kitchen and Lou remained by the cash register…the brothers still call it (the cash register) their own little Jewish Piano. Just as Nick finished checking and turning the two pizzas he had in the oven and was routinely raising the handle that would close the oven door, the kitchen seem to fill with a savage and fierce sound…as loud as an explosion in that crowded kitchen. A microsecond later…as the initial explosion was still resonating…he heard a floppy loud thud…and…a screech of automobile breaks. The pizza peel he was holding dropped out of his hand, and he didn't even realize it.

His older brother Louie…as wide-eyed and as surprised as Nick…burst into the kitchen…swinging his head to the right, to the left and back again...again and again… trying to see what caused that very loud disturbance…and almost half hissing and yelling…"What da fuck happen??? What happen…ya alright?? What happen???"

Twenty-seven and a half feet from the door of the pizzeria and in the center of Albany Street, John was struck by a vehicle traveling southeast. The force of the impact was so great he was flung, forty-six feet and six inches into the rear door panel of a parked vehicle. He just crumbled onto the wet pavement. The rain fell softly on his right cheek…a WWII scarred cheek. The force of the impact dislodged his right shoe; a laced shoe, not a loafer. The shoe came to rest against a metal garbage can on the sidewalk directly across the street from Pescatore's Albany Street entrance, the one that had a professional hand painted sign (Vascara's Signs) running along the bottom edge. The sign read; **No shoes…No shirt…NO SERVICE!!!**

Johnny…(young Johnny…old Johnny) was a good kid; the family… everybody…liked him: he was quiet, obedient, good looking and a hard worker. Calls were made. The family…those available and nearby, gathered…"How bad is it???" "What can I do for you???"..."Ya need anything???" "Who can I call??…Ya need anything…??? Ya sure…?"…"Oh God!!! Oh God….please help him…please help him…Whadda the cops say???" "Johnny is a piece of bread…a piece of bread!!!"

"He was coming back from Pesky's…he bought pizza for his mom and Linda…Oh God…Oh God…don't abandon him….help him, help him, piece of bread!!!…PLEASE, somebody that good…that considerate…that sweet…please Help him!!!"

Johnny was placed on the operating table in the hospital that had a cloth sheet upon a paper sheet protecting its plastic vinyl upholstery. There were two nurses, a female intern and an MD busily working on him. "Don't worry about his other shoe…get his jacket and shirt off…looks like internal bleeding…Hey!!!…I know him…it is Johnny Dee…I went to school with one of his younger sisters…Oh God…Oh God…that's for later…now take his valuables back to the reception desk…get more number two type bandages and a couple boxes of gauze…what's his heart rate??? Check his eyes….gimme a read on his pressure…"

They worked frantically. Johnny drifted quietly and slowly between a stage of semi-consciousness and total unconsciousness. In the fog of semi-consciousness, he thought of…recess at the Brandegee School playground…*Hey Johnny, how cum we sing My country tis of thee and land where my fathers died...my fadder is still livin and my grandfadder died in IT-LEE...I don't know...whaddaya tink???* Sleep and then…a mental image of La Francese…looking at him…kissing the palm of his right hand…holding it for a few seconds…looking at him…and then twisting his hand slightly and placing it on her breast…*it is soft but firm and warm!*

Johnny coughed and seemed to gag. He turned his head to the left and vomited blood. His rectal muscles relaxed, as did his sphincter; he soiled the paper sheeting that protected the tabletop. Like the bloody vomit, his body ejected blood from the rectum, and Johnny died.

Oh God!!! No!!! No!!! The family now had to make arrangements and the first thing was to call Carmine, *Father Willenburg is already here.*

The red blood that the hospital staff wiped up with the gauze and cotton was placed and (almost slammed) into a tall vertical container. It was a good three feet tall with a forty inch rim. In less than one hour, an orderly…with plastic gloves…took the large canister and dumped its contents into the basement incinerator by the boiler room. It was forty years ago…that the same red blood was spilled and absorbed into the Italian soil near Bologna. It was the same red blood which stained pieces of gauze and cotton which some army medic burned in an incinerator at an Army hospital not too far from Naples in 1944.

Backside and Underside

Pg Dn

It was very late October. Lotta things happening in Tony's life. It was like he had been on the top of a very high hill and started his descent and the closer he got to the bottom of the hill, the faster he seemed to be going. Too fast…he did not want to go that fast…not now…things were falling off…you forget…postponing…you procrastinate…you change things and later question your decision…too fast. A couple of visits to the Emergency Room this year made him promise his wife and kids that he would cut down his drinking. Sometimes, the wine and the bourbon would slow things down a little bit…or he'd like to think so.

November is coming...in a couple of days...today the sky is gray and looks so heavy…lead...maybe a shovel full of wet cement...heavy…he had just put a CD into his computer…Tchaikovsky…1812 Overture…Ma used to say, "You always know where you were born, but you'll never know where you will die". Yeah, Ma used to always say that…and Ma didn't like November or December because it got dark so much earlier…she would worry about kids in the dark…kids should be in the nest at night…safe…the darkness hides so much…maybe too much…you gotta be extra careful in the darkness.

Tony always liked this Tchaikovsky piece, he made it a point to listen for the bells…he felt that the bells in middle of an artillery barrage were like an unexpected promise of hope…something that told you, "Hang in there it is going to be alright…just a little more…it'll be alright". And, boy, with that gray and gloomy sky… he needed that promise of hope now.

November….no wonder it is called "il messe delle morti" (the month of the dead). It was bad timing, he had to…**he just had to**…start working on that file. He had come to call it The Melchoirre File. Over that past year and half, he had just pussyfooted around it…always some excuse…more research…read that book…read this article…*are YOU sure about this...how 'bout dat... ya sure??? NO!!! NOW*…pick up the file and start to work, close it, rest, start again…*ya gotta start and you gotta finish...you gotta Alpha and Omega this damn thing...get it off of your back*. It must not go back into the darkness…to be forgotten like childhood wishes. *Don't let it be forgotten.*

The file and its contents will tell the story…the 624 page book will document the history…*it is all there!!!* He knew the hard copy spoke with the truth of the written word. Tony assured himself of that, but then added, as if in prayer, *Sweet Jesus...let me do right by this...stay with me...I gotta tell the soft underside of the story...the way Joey would want it told and the way YOU allowed it to happen...(maybe).*

Tony remembered what seemed like a hundred years ago when he was taking a course in college, at night and way before he married. The English Lit class was discussing Steinbeck's *Grapes of Wrath* and as with Faulkner's small dog in his short story, *The Bear*, Steinbeck's turtle in the *Grapes,* had a story to tell…sometimes with a multi-layered meaning. It always amazed Tony how those masters created those masterpieces in so few paragraphs and pages. The masters could describe a scene or a thought…or make an observation and it would open up a whole panorama of feelings, of emotions, of fears and of hope.

Was the turtle a metaphor of the agonizing trek to California and the hardships faced once there…remember how hard he struggled when he was on his back in the middle of the road? What was Faulkner's little cur saying about how to be brave? But, of course, he was…still he didn't even know if he would be able to get into heaven…***because they have already decided that I don't possess an immortal soul.***

Tony picked up the file once more and he was determined to tell the story the way that Joey would want it told and the way that, maybe, God allowed it to happen.

Pg Up

The Soft Underside…

It was one of those July days when it was much better to play softball as soon as the Brandegee Playground opened at nine AM than in the afternoon. It was gonna be a scorcher just like yesterday. The sky was pale blue and none of the guys could remember if they saw a cloud yesterday either. They sure as hell ain't gunna see any clouds today. Frankie Lo Conto banged one off of the Brandegee School Gymnasium wall (classrooms were on the second floor) straight down the left field line, high up…almost to the classroom windows and very, very deep early in the game. They knew that hit was going to be the benchmark for the rest of the summer and many more summers to come.

Angela, Nunzio's sister, came walking quickly…almost running…and stopped on the first base line. She fanatically motioned with her right arm to her brother who was playing shortstop, and with just her lips said, "Come!!! Come quick…hurry…come!!!" Her brother knotted his eyebrows and angrily glared at his sister for being so bold as to interrupt their game. He was about to send her home, but before he could, he noticed the desperation and urgency of his younger sister's actions.

He thought…*It's bad….It must be sumptin' bad…I gotta go!!! I gotta go NOW!!!!*

He pulled off his glove, one of only three baseball gloves shared by both teams, tossed it to Jap Grande (he was elected team captain that day) and without saying a word, first walked very quickly, then trotted and by the time he crossed the imaginary left field foul line he was sprinting. Both he and Angela ran as fast as they could back to the Melchiorre house. It wasn't far away…at the far end of the schoolyard…just on the other side of the school's cyclone fence.

All the guys watched like frozen statues as brother and sister disappeared into the womb of the 'mother' Melchiorre house. Every one of them wondered what had happened…"It musta been…hadda be important…didcha see how fast Nunzie ran?"

In a minute or two, Jap finally said to Bobby Giruzzi (the other team captain), "Okay….youse guys gotta catch fur us…Fat Tony…you gotta play short….and youse guys catching, no dirty stuff…play the game the right way."

Playing short made Tony a little uncomfortable, he would worry about timing, his jump if a line came off of the bat…or worse yet…a ground ball going through your legs (*dat was the worst!*) or being too slow moving to the right or the left…all that stuff. He put on the glove and went out to play short.

Tony remembered a lotta things about that day in July, 1950. He remembered and could still see Frankie Lo Conto's beautiful Joe Di Maggio swing and the ball bouncing off of the wall right under the classroom window. He remembered and could still see Nunzio and Angela running home, and he could remember and still see that high, outside fastball Bobby Bucerrio pitched to him. He saw the ball leave Bobby's hand. He twisted his shoulders and turned his back to the pitcher, never taking his eye off of the softball coming to him. Like a spring unwinding, his shoulders started twisting forward, his arms extended, his right knee seemed to bend just a bit, his right foot pushed down hard on the grassless playground dirt, his eyes glued to the point where the ball collided with his taped-up baseball bat, his body uncoiling, coming around with beast-like strength…and he forced the baseball in the other direction.

Tony had swung a fraction of a second late…he almost took the ball out of the catchers out spread hands…and set it flying to right field. The ball soared over the first baseman's head, over the sidewalk that ran the length of Catherine Street, over Catherine Street itself, over the weedy pathway (Was it a sidewalk? No one ever seemed to walk on that side of the street.), barely clearing the six-foot cyclone fence around N.D. Peters Cement yard and into the 'skyscrapers of cement blocks'.

Luckily, the guys saw an employee of N.D. Peters walking in the general area and asked him to retrieve the ball. Had it not been for him, it would have meant climbing the fence. By the time their only softball was in their control again, the heat…the mystery about Nunzio…the display of baseball power…it was all too much…the guys called it a day.

Tony always knew…he just know…that as well as he connected on Bobby Bucerrio's high, outside fastball, his hit never traveled the distance that Frankie got. For a while…a short while because Frankie went on to become one of those three letter sports stars…some of the guys said the Tony's hit and Frankie's hit were equal distance. Tony was not going to challenge anything, he was secretly delighted that he was able to clear the fence and thought, *Dats all right…it was my best…and I ain't never…ever… gunna do any better dan dat*…and he'd always remember it as such.

To the day, just a month before Frankie's incredible smash to right field and Tony's late swing with a taped bat and the ball falling in amid the cement blocks 'skyscrapers, something was happening in the outside world. In a world that was not really theirs.

The Hard Cold Crust of Documentation...the Backside
Utica Observe~Dispatch

Vol. 29___NO.56 14 PAGES UTICA, N. Y., MONDAY EVENING , JUNE 26, 1950 PRICE FIVE CENTS

and then above this newspaper mast head and across six of the eight columns
in inky black bold #30 pica:, it read:

RED TANKS JAB NEAR SEOUL

And another

IN MORTAL COMBAT...KOREA 1950~1953
By John Toland
Chapter 1 A Time of War
(June 24-25, 1950)

On the murky night of June 24, 1950, Soviet 122-mm howitzers, 76-mm guns, and self-propelled guns, were already emplaced taking the 38th parallel. One hundred fifty Russian-built T-34 tanks were cautiously moving forward to their final attack positions along with 90,000 combat troops, all trained by soviet military advisers. The Korean People's Army was poised for its surprise invasion of the south.

On the other side of the 38th parallel, four understrength Republic of Korea divisions and one regiment were on the front lines...

(and more)...Enlisted ROK soldiers from farming villages had recently been given fifteen–day leaves to help their families with the crops. Already outnumbered, the ROK front line that night was dangerously depleted.

Page 23

(and still another)

Fifty to sixty years later, if you were to surf: koreanwar-educator.org. You would get a twenty three page print out entitled:

A BRIEF HISTORY OF THE KOREAN WAR
PACIFIC STARS & STRIPES

An editor's note/recognition/disclaimer and then
THE WAR IN KOREA – JUNE 25, 1950 TO MARCH 1953
Page one- paragraphs two, three and four:

First Untied States troops rushed to the battle zone from Japan in early July, 1950, were from the 24th Infantry Division. "Task Force Smith", commanded by Lt. Col. Charles B. Smith, consisted of elements of Companies B, and C, 21st Infantry Regiment, a battery of 105 howitzers from the 52nd Field

Artillery Battalion, plus some mortars, 2.36-inch bazookas, and recoilless Rifles, reached Pusan on July 2, 1950, and moved up to meet the Korean

Communist forces pouring down from the north. Overwhelming numbers of well–armed, well trained North Korean soldiers, spearheaded by Russian-made T-34 tanks, hit the small U.S. force on the morning of July 5 and forced a withdrawal. By this time, other elements of the 24th had reached Korea and joined "Task Force Smith" its efforts to the North Korean advance.

The enemy was demonstrating surprising strength by this time. He had plenty of tanks, artillery, and mortars; his infantry was well–trained, tough and aggressive, and his tactics were well-planned and executed. In the face of this superiority in numbers, and offensive weapons, U.S. troops fought back valiantly, withdrawing only when threatened with encirclement and making the enemy pay for every inch of yielded ground.

These delaying tactics gained time for the arrival of other U.S. units in Korea and while the enemy was not stopped, he was forced to slow down his timetable, which called for seizure of the entire peninsula within weeks of his first break across the 38th parallel.

The Soft Underside

Faustine Melchiorre never married. She was the oldest daughter of Angelo and Maria Melchiorre. For no apparent reason, (or so it seemed to Tony anyway) it seemed many of the first-born females of large households remained chaste. Tony speculated maybe it was that they saw how very hard mothers had to work. Later in life, Tony figured maybe they either worshiped their fathers or subconsciously despised them, thus remaining celibate to help protect the mother from the Alpha of the pack. *Aaahey!!!* Tony thought *Leave dat heavy stuff to Sigmund Freud.*

Faustine (and all the others followed) was the first of the Melchiorre's to be born in the 'Melchiorre House' and that was late in the first decade of the Twentieth Century. Cosmo and Gaetano were born elsewhere: Cosmo three months before Ellis Island and Gaetano in Ohio at Maria's older brother's house.

In *le Stati Uniti* (the United States) one bright Sunday morning, a young strong Angelo, who could read just a little bit, and his pregnant wife Maria (who could not read even a little) with their two sons and all their worldly possessions left Ohio, boarded a train and came to Utica. When they walked to and from the train stations, Maria, of course, struggled much more with her burden than her mate; but did not complain. In her past, present and future life, hardships were the rule and the exception.

Each carried a son, and Angelo also carried a rather large bundle…the bundle held their worldly possessions, and Maria, carried an old used flour sack containing a loaf of bread, a grapefruit sized piece of provolone, and a small jug of wine. Several times Angelo would straddle his eldest son across the back of his neck, with the child's legs dangling from his father's shoulders, and voluntarily lighten Maria's load by carrying the provisions.

The young family was now on their own. Going to a new city, in a new country, to build a family, and build a future. They moved into the N. D. Peters building (aka Melchiorre house) first floor front. The wooden door to the cold water flat had a metal number "one" nailed into it at about eye level, and next to it a metal capital 'W'. It meant 'west' (occidente) and Angelo…who could read just a little…did not recognize the letter 'W'.

In 1950, Faustine was still working at the Oneida Knitting Mills. She had considered herself 'lucky' to find work there late in the thirties. Sure, at first, it was only a couple of mornings a week, then two or three days a week, and then the war came, and they had all the work you wanted. It was only two blocks from the front stoop to the time clock.

Once Tony, Nunzio and Buster were taking turns carrying an old automobile tire they had found to a junkyard, because they were positive they could get a least a quarter for it. They walked past the Oneida factory on Broad Street. From one of the third floor windows of the shop they saw someone waving to them. It was Faustine waving to her brother.

In early July of that year, shortly after the Fourth of July, Faustine came home from work at the usual time. Her mother was cooking and their flat smelled of greens. The working men in the household were not home yet. The days were longer and the construction crews were getting in and hour or two of extra work. Her mother said there was a letter on the dresser that came today and she thought it might be from Joe. *Who else would be writing*???

Hat Box Becky's Forgiveness

Pg Dn

Yeah!!! What else could it be? Other than the wine or being half in the bag!!! Tony was having 'good and evil' discussion with himself and he struck upon "forgiveness"…don't ask him why…he just did. *A drunk is a forgiving guy…*the good said to him, but quickly, the evil retorted…*dat ain't true…ya know and remember a lotta of nasty and very unforgiving drunks…*then the poor 'good' thought a moment, and said nothing.

Tony took another sip of the Chianti … quickly sealed his lips, swirled the 'grape' around…over and under his tongue onto his gums…then popped his lips open let the air in and swallowed. *Dats the way yur supposed to do it if'n you wanna see if itz good stuff…well??? Whadda about forgiveness? I don't know…just don't know!!!*

*Christ forgave…He always did!!! Yeah I know…but he wasn't a drunk…*a pensive moment of deep thought…*Yeah I know but maybe he didn't hafta drink!!!*

Pg Up

Tony's feelings were hurt, they…some of the older kids…and even two of his cousins…but mostly the older boys…started to taunt him because he could not climb the rear rigging of the billboard on Broad Street. The others seemed to climb it effortlessly and were already up high, near the top and Tony was struggling so. In what proved to be his final attempt, he ripped out the seat of his pants. His contemporaries roared with laughter and some started to call him Fatso and Tubby Wubby.

Tony left the weedy vacant lot, which was almost the size of a city block and had two billboards on either end, a very large Dutch Elm (near the bakery) and a small tree behind the Ritrona house, off of Pelletteri Ave. He went quickly because he didn't wish to be seen half exposed and endure more humiliation.

He burst out at a full run when he reached the alleyway, scampered up the four cement steps of the back alley stoop and rushed up the sixteen steps to their flat; *second floor rear.* Ma and his cousin Antoinette were washing clothes.

That, the washing of clothes, was a monumental task in those days, almost an all day process. First, the women had to steer and jockey the Maytag upright washing machine out of the *stanza vacanta* (vacant room). Ma always had it covered with an old bedspread when in storage…to keep it new. Then, they would position the machine …with those two very dangerous lethal white rollers…near the kitchen sink. There were four drains in the flat: the toilet, the bathroom sink, the bathtub and finally, the kitchen sink.

The bathroom was much too small to accommodate the two operators and the large four-legged white monster. The pivot arm on the top housed the two unforgiving and dangerous rollers…*dat could pull ya in dare and squeeze the guts otta ya…*directly above the machine's large wash tub. Beneath the tub was a big black unseen motor (protected and covered by fenders) that provided the electrical power to twist and swirl the machine's agitator, rotate the squeezing rollers and work the pump to empty the tub. All the women Tony knew were deathly afraid of those wringers. They acted accordingly when the wringers were engaged and it was easy to sense their concentration on the task, especially during the wringing cycle of the wash.

They also had to fill the washtub with hot water from the kitchen sink (after they had lit the gas on the hot water tank a half hour before).

"Tony whadda ya doin home??? Why aren't ya out playing?" they both kind of asked.

"Aahh I don't know Ma…I don't want to."

Tony knew that Ma and Antoinette were much too busy to pay attention to him.

"Ma…Ma. I ripped my pants again…" he knew she would be angry, but not as angry now because she was watching those rollers. She was feeding the clothes out of the tub into the mouth of the rollers and Antoinette was catching on the other side. They were wide-eyed and engrossed in this stage of it, for if…*God forbid*…anything would happen, either or both would quickly reach up on top of the roller unit and hit the leveler arm which would put the roller in reverse and then, eventually stop it.

The rollers made a whirling noise when engaged.

"Ma???" he paused a bit…no response from ether of the working women… "Nan???…Ma??? The utter kids were calling me names…"

Antoinette had just successfully retrieved a squeezed-out tee shirt from the jaws of the wringers and was snapping some of the excess moisture from it. Ma, head down, looking into the machine's tub, found another tee shirt and fished it out and quickly started to hand wring it. Antoinette wanted to give the little boy some attention, for she too had often been shamed by her peers. "Whadda dey call ya???"

"Aahh nuttin…things like fatso and tubby wubby…stuff like dat."

Ma was starting to put the soaking tee shirt in the wringer and as she did said to Antionette, "Donetta stata attenda (stay alert)." Unblinking, she watched the rollers take the wet shirt, compress the water from it, and without taking her eyes off of her (their) dangerous rotating rollers, replied to her socially injured son, to retort by calling them a bag of skin and bones.

Antoinette, too, had a come back for him to use… "All ya gotta do… is say …sticks and stones will break my bones…but names will never hurt me."

Yeah dats right!!! Sticks and ***especially stones*** *will break anybody's bones...dats for sure!!!*

That Sunday he went to St. Anthony's church with his father and Uncle Dan. His father would always give him a nickel or sometimes a dime to put into the basket at collection. He really didn't like to go to the ten o'clock mass because most of the time it would be three priests (a High Mass) and it seemed to take so much longer than the seven o'clock...normal...mass. His mind fueled by impatience and boredom and childish daydreaming would usually wander far and wide.

But not this time.

The sermon was about bunch of guys who were going to throw stones at this woman...for something bad she did...and Jesus or God told them...go ahead if YOU never sinned yourself.

...and over the many years...Tony never forgot that Sunday morning sermon....as time passed and as his sins and those that sinned against him...would become recalled...in the crevices and dark corner of his mind...the awaiting sinner would always be a different person...but never himself...

...because he knew... he himself was a stone thrower...at times he really didn't want to be one who cast stones...but he was and when not casting stones at others...he was indulging himself and wallowing in his own self pity.

Pg Dn

....surreal...

She was standing, her head was down and her eyes tightly closed. She was clutching a small dresser lamp that had no lamp shade and depicted a pair of shapely woman's dancing legs with a tutu and a circular blue base beneath the dancer's legs. Her chin was pressing hard down deep into her throat and neck, and her shoulders were hunched upward as if she were anticipating a blow from a switch. Her head appeared to be shrinking deeper and deeper into her body. She had never experienced such shame and humiliation, nor such bitter regret and profound sorrow.

She stood there…letting the newfound silence engulf her…but it was not a peaceful silence, it was the silence of anxious anticipation, of stinging pain. She awaited an unwelcome death…as all deaths are….and she was told it was for all those past sins…but it did not abate that trembling fear of inevitable pain.

A soothing voice drifted into the silence…"Rebecca"…and it was said in Yiddish, as she remembered her grandfather calling her name out. Still afraid and still very humiliated and shameful, Becky did not open her eyes. The voice called her again and seemed just a tad more gentle and understanding…"Rebecca"…and this time she also heard the wind whispering as it ruffled the leaves of the nearby tree. She slowly opened her eyes.

For a long moment, she just stared at the grassless and crusted ground at her feet, for her shame did not yet allow her to raise her head. Slowly, she swung her head to the left and then to the right, revealing the same grassless and crusty soil. She now raised her head and through squinting eyes did a 180-degree peek at the barren panorama before her…barren…neither man nor beast. Slightly behind her and to the right stood a huge fig tree and the soft breeze played its concert by rustling through the leaves. The remainder was as barren as the terrain to her front.

"Becky"…the familiar voice came from near the tree…but she saw no one… "Becky"…the voice repeated.

Becky simply replied…"Yes Grandpa"

"Where are they? They who have condemned you and wish to stone you? Where are they???"

Rebecca looked around once more, seeing only the same barren landscape with a solitary but massive fig tree. "They have all gone…no one is here Grandpa."

Pg Dn

Big John is a retired railroad man, having given the New York Central and Amtrak almost forty-three years of work, just a few more than had his father a generation before. He, like Tony and others of that generation, were happy in their retirement…and almost in chorus you could hear them all say…"I do what I wanna do and not what I gotta do…or…every day is Saturday and I'll do it NEXT Saturday!!" John and a retired fireman opened a used furniture store, and dabbled a bit in buying used gold and *udder stuff*…but definitely excluding any illegal drugs and related paraphernalia. "Whadda ya nuts or sumptin?? Whadda I wanna get mixed up in that shit for???" And he did not…ever. The retired fireman soon became disenchanted and sought a warmer climate in the south. Big John bought his half for…like he was fond of saying…A song and a dance.

John set his own hours, to match his leisure lifestyle, and soon developed a rapidly forming circle of friends, of buying and selling clients and associates that were the denizens of the deep…and the saints and sinners. The store was a haven for all of God's creatures and if truth be known, "nary" a stone caster in the bunch. The location of the store pleased Tony very much. And why shouldn't it? There it was right smack in the center of his childhood neighborhood…and all the props to trigger or jump start his memories from those days so long ago.

Like most used furniture stores and because of its size, there was not that much used or new furniture, but it was incredibly cluttered. Near the front door was a glass encased counter, with three shelves all overflowing with used wrist watches, pens, jack knives, pins and broaches and bracelets and costume jewelry. Narrow foot paths…passageways…snaked around tons of electronic equipment, sneakers, clothes racks, table lamps, CD's, hand tools, electric tools, seldom used exercise equipment and the occasional lawn mower or two, used computers, monitors, miles of connecting cables, printers…and on and on, and in the rear of the store, right on the other side of a shaky wall petition, was a small three by two room that housed a toilet. Near the door to the bathroom was a deep maintenance sink with two floor mops propped therein…standing at attention and guarding the bathroom door. There were shelves over the maintenance tub that had an ample supply of toilet paper and paper towel rolls.

A small dormitory sized refrigerator was strategically placed between the cluttered desk and the equally cluttered 'jewelry counter'. The fridge was far from empty and just as cluttered. At times Big John could negotiate for frozen or fresh meats…and shrimp and maybe lobster...and at other times…not.

The last time Tony was there, he was offered…and immediately accepted…a beer and a Di Napoli Tuscany cigar. Immensely enjoying both, he casually watched the blue-gray smoke drift upwards to the tin ceiling above and slowly dissipate. Lowering his eyes he looked out the big store front window and noticed a city bus rumbling to a stop to take on passengers and then start up with a jerk and roll forward toward Genesee Street. As the bus floated out of his field of vision, Tony noticed a young black, maybe Hispanic, boy walking his dog on the other side of the street.

The dog was a pit bull and he was quick stepping enough so as to keep the leash taunt. The boy had a baseball hat on his head, with the visor at a rakish angle over his left ear; he was shirtless, wore long basketball shorts, with his underwear showing above his waist line, and ankle high sneakers with no visible socks. He swaggered a bit. As if to say…*Hey look at me! I got this pit bull…the dog of choice of drug dealers…got these cool sneakers and no socks…my shorts are satin and shiny black with white piping…clinging low on my hips…enough underwear showing to make me super cool!!!* He strutted and swaggered out of Tony's field of vision.

Tony took another drag on his cigar and watched the blue gray smoke start its upward drift. And he thought…*Maybe I didn't look like that, but I know I felt like that…like I was somebody…and wanted the world to know it!…with a pocket full of dreams!* Then he noticed the big puff of smoke had dissipated.

Tony thought of an appropriate adage, *The more things change, the more they stay the same.*

MELCHIORRIE
JOSEPH
RA121165
T50
MELCHIOR
JOSEPH
RA12116598
T50 AB
ROMAN CATHOLIC

Land That I Love

The Oldest Girl

The oldest girl in the Melchiorre family was named Faustine. To Tony, it seemed that so many of the eldest (first born females) in those large Italian families, never married. *Dats fur sure!!! Yeah...sure! Look at Zia Maria Nicola in It-lee...she had ten kids...TEN!!!...five boys...five girls...all of da boys dat lived (four of 'em) married...and not one...not one of da girls ever got married...Lizetta the oldest...stayed home and da utter four sisters all became nuns...nuns like in sister schools...dat kind of nun!* Tony often wondered about this perceived phenomenon, and thought…was it fear or was it love that kept the eldest in the nest.

Faustine never married; but she always worked.

Faustine quit school early, or as soon as she could back in those days. In the summer when she was much younger, she'd pick beans and she'd help watch and raise the younger siblings. Eventually, during WWII, she found work in one of the textile mills (the Oneida Knitting Mills) and worked there until they, the mills, moved south in the sixties. Years later, a term was coined reflecting the early sixties and the exodus of the textile industry from Utica (probably the entire northeast): from loom to doom.

Her world was small. On work days, she'd walk east on Catherine Street to Tony Marraffa's fish store on the corner, left onto Kossuth Avenue…a short city block…cross Broad Street…down the employee alley to the employee entrance and to the time clock. That time clock, with its large hinged arm on the right like the slots in Vegas, was the one that she and the others pulled twice a workday. Put your card in the narrow slot…card number 303…pull the arm downward…a bell would ring somewhere inside the belly of the time clock; and when you lifted the card out of the slot, you could see…in a sort of faded red ink "6:49 A", or "6:52 A", or whatever. The

‘A’ was for AM. Punching out, the letter was ‘P’ and nobody really knew why the M was never shown.

And on the real hot days in July and August, management would give you salt tablets if you wanted them. And, on those real cold January and February days it was a good idea to wear a heavy sweater; some of the girls never took off their coats.

Her world was small. On Saturday, there were thousands of household chores to do. However, at times, there might be a wedding at De Rosa Hall on Bleecker Street (never during Lent) or maybe a movie on Saturday night at the Rialto or Family Theater. Sunday was sort of a relaxed day, if relaxed is the right word. Faustine, her Mom and all the other girls would go to the seven o’clock mass at Our Lady of Mount Carmel. The men in the family…those that went to church…would go to a later Mass.

Her young brothers, Joey and Alfred and Nunzio and Junior were pretty good about going every Sunday, but the much older boys seldom went. They gained a sort of independence after serving in the army, and although Mom campaigned to get them back in the pre-WWII discipline, she was never successful. Pa did not push. And now, Joey was in the army and stationed in far away Japan, he just turned twenty on his last birthday.

Shortly before the Fourth of July vacation day in 1950, she received a letter from Joey, sent from far away Japan. Japan, she thought, was not too far from Korea…*was it?* There seemed to a lot of news about Korea in the newspapers and on the radio these days.

The letter was formatted and indented exactly the way Mrs. Bailey and Miss Hall and Mrs. Martin taught their classes at Brandegee School. Date and time in the upper right hand corner, the salutation on the near left and the first sentence of each paragraph indented one half inch and the other lines directly under the “Dear” of the salutation.

The soft underside…the written words of saints and heroes…the stamped printed words of rules and regulations.

June 25th 1950
Sunday nite
9:30 p.m.

Dear Sis,

Just a few lines to let you know that I am feeling fine and hope to hear the same from you and the family.

Sis no doubt you have heard what has happened today. About North Korea, attacking South Korea. Sis don't worry it will be alright. I am alright we have not been affected by what has happened.

I was on guard today. I was on guard last nite at 4:30 and got off at 6:30. It rained out here all day today and yesterday we were alerted for a typhoon. Although thank God it did not get this far.

A week ago Friday we went to Hakkatta for 5 days. We had a couple of problems to run out there. It was something for a change. We had a [illegible]

II

time. We slept near a beach.
So the way we washed up in
the morning. We used to jump
in the water. It was salt water
so it didn't do much good but
wake us up. All we did most
of the time was swim
and lay around the beach.
I got a nice sun tan out
of the deal. We are supposed
to go back to the same spot
July 17th. We are supposed to
stay for 14 days this time.
Rose sent me a medal
for my birthday. I got it yesterday. I had it blessed today.

Sis I am sorry that this
is so short. But it is time
for lights to go out. I'll write
more soon. Don't worry I
am alright. Love to the family
Regards to Aunt Rosie & Rosie
Click.

Love
"Joey"

Text of Joey's Letter

June 25th 1950
Sunday Night
9:30 p m

Dear Sis,

Just a few lines to let you know that I am feeling fine and hope to hear the same from you and the family. Sis, no doubt you have heard what has happened today – North Korea, attacking South Korea. Sis don't worry it will be alright. I am alright. We have not been affected by what has happened. I was on guard today. I went on guard last night at 4:30 and got off at 6:30. It rained out here all day today and yesterday and we were alerted for a typhoon. Although, thank God, it did not get this far. A week ago Friday we went to Haklakatta for 5 days. We had a couple of problems to run out there. It was something for a change. We had a good

(next page)

time. We slept near a beach. So, to wash up in the morning, we just jumped in the water. It was saltwater, so it didn't do much good but it did wake us up. All we did most of the time was swim and lay around the beach. I got a nice suntan out of the deal. We are supposed to go back to the same spot July 17th and stay for 14 days this time. Dorie sent me a medal for my birthday. I got it yesterday. I had it blessed today. Sis, I am sorry that this is so short. It is time for the lights to go out. I'll write more soon. Don't worry, I am alright. Love to the family. Regards to Aunt Rosie & Rosie Click.

Love,
"Joey"

The soft underside

"NO!!!!" Mr. Louie cursed under his breath, "NO!!!"

"NO…damn the rules and regulations! Damn 'em! This will go out tomorrow…it'll be time enough…we cannot change anything now…why give these the poor souls more to worry about this night? Yes…give 'em a less stressful night…tomorrow…I'll be in early and take care of it…"

"Le Roy," he called out, "Paste this…stamp it…and give right back to me."

Le Roy obeyed.

The kindly old Mr. Louie, who is not too far from retirement now, seated at his regional manager's desk, reached into his right front vest pocket and pulled out a set of keys. He flopped them in his right hand, spotted the one he needed…it was easy…it was the smallest key on the double ringed keychain, and opened the middle desk drawer. He sighed sadly and laid the telegram in the center of the drawer, right on top of all those other supposedly important papers and slid the drawer shut. *Hail Mary full of grace, the lord is…*

Yes…Tomorrow…not now…it is late…the poor souls are worried and stressed out enough…let 'em have a just a piece more of what…less worry? Yeah less worry…this will only make the worry heavier…tomorrow….time enough tomorrow…

The hard backside…the printed word.

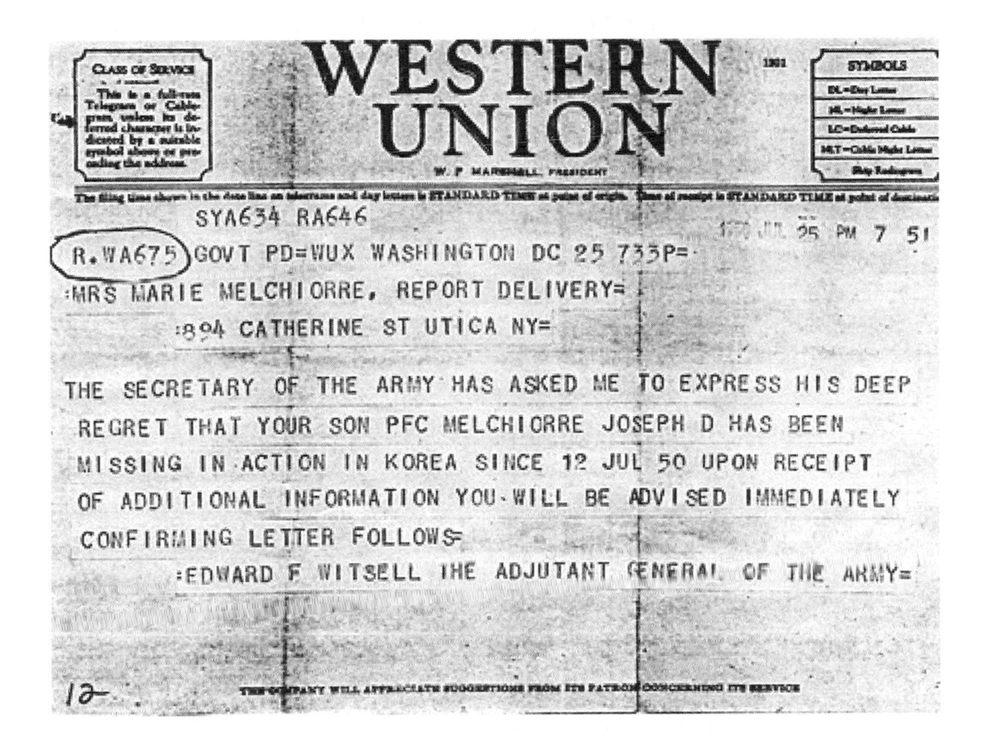

WESTERN UNION

W. P. MARSHALL, PRESIDENT

SYA634 RA646

1950 JUL 25 PM 7 51

R.WA675 GOVT PD=WUX WASHINGTON DC 25 733P=

:MRS MARIE MELCHIORRE, REPORT DELIVERY=

:894 CATHERINE ST UTICA NY=

THE SECRETARY OF THE ARMY HAS ASKED ME TO EXPRESS HIS DEEP REGRET THAT YOUR SON PFC MELCHIORRE JOSEPH D HAS BEEN MISSING IN ACTION IN KOREA SINCE 12 JUL 50 UPON RECEIPT OF ADDITIONAL INFORMATION YOU WILL BE ADVISED IMMEDIATELY CONFIRMING LETTER FOLLOWS=

:EDWARD F WITSELL THE ADJUTANT GENERAL OF THE ARMY=

12

THE COMPANY WILL APPRECIATE SUGGESTIONS FROM ITS PATRONS CONCERNING ITS SERVICE

Joey…in Japan

Pg Up

The squad tent had accommodations for 12 men (an infantry squad), three double-decker bunks with green wooden footlockers on each end and a potbelly stove in the center. The stove had a small tin chimney flu that vented through the ceiling. There were upright lockers by each of the two entrances, six on either side of the door. The new guys initially always put locks on them, but in time, it wasn't worth the hassle and further, it was simply because all the guys just had to be trusted. However, unlike the upright lockers, all the footlockers had some kind of locking device…combination or key, trust does have its boundaries.

Two guys had made their way out earlier the past month and it turned out a top bunk was open on the south side of the squad tent and a bottom bunk was available by the north entrance of the tent. Nobody really wanted that bottom bunk because of the constant (or what seemed to be constant) traffic in and out of the north portal. When the two guys moved out to go home, everybody agreed including the Squad Sergeant and the First Snake (who didn't even live in that tent…but his okay was required because he had to advise the Sgt. of the location of the men's bunks for guard duty) approved of Jenkins changing bunks before the new guys transferred in. Jenkins was a good guy, from Colorado of all places, and everybody liked him.

Joey had just returned to the squad tent from Headquarters. He had gone there to mail two letters – one to home and the other to his girlfriend, Dorie. Jenkins was polishing his boots and told them that all the squad leaders and the First Snake were all at the Officers' tent being briefed.

"What's up, that Korea stuff???"

"Yeah I guess so....everybody is talking 'bout it???"

At 10:15 or 22:15 hrs in military jargon, the routine 'Lights Out' order came over the PA system from the Orderly Room, but the lights were still burning brightly at the Officers' quarters.

The squad, the companies, the whole regiment was "mustered and put on alert" at 03:30 hrs that morning. The old man came out and addressed the troops. Soon after, he told the Executive Officer, standing three paces to his rear and off to the left, to dismiss the troops. He did so by shouting the order to the Captains who were standing in front of their companies. The Captains did an about face (one hundred eighty degree turn...military jargon) faced their companies an echoed, "Company dismissed!!!"

The Platoon leaders, mostly Lieutenants, spun around in a military manner, and repeated the order to the enlisted men of the 21st Infantry Regiment on that warm June...almost July...barely dawning morning ..in 1950. The troops returned to the squad tents and proceeded to follow the orders of the Regimental Commander; they packed their gear in their duffle bags, then in military-style rotation marched to the company armoire and drew their weapons. The normal routine of noting the time, date and signature requirement was waived this budding morning...

"Whaddya tink?"

"Maybe it won't be dat bad...."

"Da radio said somebody called it a police action or sumptin...so now we're cops huh???"

"Ya can betcha Korea ain't no fuckin picnic!!!"

"Yeah, I know dat...but where in Korea?"

"How much ya gotta know bout Korea anyway? Like ya gunna find out where all the cat houses are or where they sell beer or sumptin? It'll be a while fore dat!!!"

"Whadda ya, God or sumptin??? Betcha dat dem politicians get to talking and we won't even hafta unpack our duffle bags...Betcha ya!"

The 21st got to Korea and soon moved north by train toward Taelon.

Intro to Korea....

The train stopped in the middle of what Joey thought was the edge of a muddy pool, it turned out to be a rice paddy; one of the very few he was to see in this strange land. The guys struggled a bit with their duffle bags, found a comparatively dry spot and stacked them as neatly as they could, hoping the canvas material of the bag was waterproof or, at least, water resistant. These thoughts were especially prevalent if your bag was at, or close to, the bottom of the pile. They lined up by Companies.

"Are dare any trucks or sumptin around here?? I don't see any? Dey gunna send trucks or something?" "Betcha we are gunna walk...I betcha ten bucks!"

Then they heard, "At ease in the ranks...the CO will be down in a minute...good time to light 'em up if'n you got 'em."

The Company Commander came down the ranks and stood as close to the center of the company as possible, his boots just about at the end of the rice paddy. Executive Officers called the company to attention. When they saw the CO coming down the line, a lotta the guys just flicked their cigarettes to the ground, but not all of them. Joey and Jenkins and a couple of others in the platoon merely plinked the hot embers off of the cigarette's end, re-inserted the cigarette in their mouth, blew into it slightly like a small whistle (to get the excess smoke out of it) and then returned the 'used' cigarette to the pack. Most of the guys smoked Camels or Luckies, very few Chesterfields.

Joey 'learned' to smoke after he got to Japan and he just realized, he never told Dorie that he was now a smoker.

Jenkins would always think and sometimes say aloud, “Waste not, want not” like his mother would always say. His mom didn’t know he smoked either.

The CO told the troops they were to move north. “Bring your field pack, two days C rations, bandoleer for each rifleman; each company has the CO’s jeep with additional ammo and supplies. The medics will move up after they stow and secure the duffle bags, with the exec’s jeep. We’ll form up behind ‘A’ company and will be moving out in ten minutes.”

“Whadda tell ya, we’re walking!!!”

“Anybody know, or ever hear of Osan???”

“Quiet in the ranks,” a sergeant ordered.

A Long Way from Home
December 1950 Camp Five

Pg Dn

Cursed with being a very slow reader…in his frustratingly long search to figure out the reason why it took him so long to finish a book…he eventually found an acceptable answer…a conclusion…sort of…and it came to the him late in life…it was simply his attention span was limited. Tony, almost unwittingly, found another excellent reference book. The book is entitled, *Remembered Prisoners of a Forgotten WAR,* by Lewis H. Carlson. The book jacket told him it was….AN ORAL HISTORY OF KOREAN WAR POWS.

Although, as he well recalled (it wasn't that long ago either!!!), he'd sworn up and down to God he would not be distracted and would plunge ahead and finish the project. But now, he'd have to read this new find first. The glaring and simple fact remained that in this work references are made to Major John J. Dunn. Let it go*….No…NO…maybe I'll learn more…*ya know 'nuff…its gunna burn up more time*…I don't care…I owe it to Joey…the Melchiorre family…*NO, don't do it…*but it ain't right* …itz yur funeral!!

He thought of Nunzio and Faustine and that large family…all of them...those that remain and those that are now gone. He thought of that dreaded file folder with the name Melchiorre Papers scrawled across its face. A letter…***that letter***…the one sent so long ago to 894 Catherine Street and dated October 30, 1953 was there inside the file. It urged him forward and repelled him at the same time.

Tony's mind just raced and struggled, and as is true of all such mental struggles, the questions outnumber anything that he could explain. *That blasted letter!!!…Who raised the question of Joey's loyalty??? Why would anyone do so???*...the Major seemed to know a lot about Joey…most of it making sense… "…he died a martyr to the cause in the fight against communism…" Maybe somebody told this Major to write 461 such letters (*Poor bastard...how easy was that to do???*) Maybe back in those troubled times, (*But times are always troubled...aren't they???*) people thought it necessary. But, he didn't have to tell any of us that…Joey Firpo Melchiorre…that we "…should be proud of him…" and he was "…a real soldier and a fine American…and you can be proud him…" and the letter…***that letter***…signed by John J. Dunn and sent to Joey's family. It told them nothing of what they really wondered about and was filled with the things that they already knew.

A Major John Dunn was also mentioned in an *Observer-Dispatch* report of Joey Melchiorre being MIA…way back on July 12, 1950. The Major was again mentioned by John Toland in his work, *In Mortal Combat Korea 1950-1953.* All of them stated Dunn was from Rome, New York. Rome…Rome New York…only sixteen miles West of Utica...only sixteen miles from Catherine Street…sixteen miles from the Melchiorre House.

There was now no doubt in Tony's mind that this Major John J. Dunn was there…and survived.

Ya gotta read it…ya gotta tell the reader…It ain't right to ignore this window…this ORAL HISTORY…but…but remember!!! There are some things you will never know…

Pg Up

Soft Underside of Reality

Marching…marching…moving…moving…he looked up ahead and it appeared that the crest of this hill was maybe a hundred yards away. *Good...good...thank God*…it was always just a little bit easier walking downhill.

He had, up until today, always helped others when there was a steep incline. Way back at the onset of the march, even when it was just as bad as this stretch, he would even support men going downhill. However, each day since, it would be less and it had now come to the point that he himself was struggling to keep in step.

The talk was, the guards would shoot those that dropped out.

And like all 'talk', there was also talk that there'd be a few carts coming up from the rear to pick up all the stragglers to bring them to the nearby dispensaries or to the next camp. It is what you wanted to believe. But today, Joey hoped that the latter was true. He could not remember when he had slept for more than two hours straight and last night he wasn't sure if he had slept at all. No sleep and it was getting so cold, especially at night. He wanted to…he really wanted to…but his body would not…could not…let him help the others. Each step forward required all of his strength and focus. At the crest of the hill, the column took a break. They were told to remain standing, and Joey wondered why. It seemed needlessly cruel.

Then, down at the far end of the column, he noticed two guards…one he recognized to be the one the guys called "Karen"…stop momentarily in front of each man, reach up towards their throat and quickly yank. "Whadda dey doin???"

"Da bastards are pulling da dog tags!!!" someone said up the line.

Joey quietly slipped one of his hands from his pants pocket, reached under his HBT fatigue shirt and tugged, snapping the chain of his Miraculous Medal of Our Lady of Fatima. He gathered the medal in his fist and put his hand back into his pocket for warmth. It was the chain Dorie sent for his birthday late in May of this year. He knew the guards would take it from him along with the tags. He didn't want those SOBs to have it because it came from Dorie, and home. Home...Home...what a nice word!!!

Not so long afterwards, near the perimeter fence of the camp, Joey ended up negotiating a trade – the necklace and medal for three apples. He had bartered this deal with a skinny little Korean girl from a nearby village. He gave two apples to the men who shared his hutch and the other he ate himself. He ate it slowly, savoring each mouthful, chewing thoughtfully and thoroughly. He experienced a fleeting moment of guilt about trading off what he had so treasured as a touchstone...a final remembrance...of home, but he knew that both God and Dorie understood.

The prisoners of war up there by the Yalu River were all very hungry and very cold. Many of them, especially those captured in July, were poorly clad for their current environment.

Hard Backside of Reality

Remembered Prisoners of a Forgotten War, L H. Carlson, page 82
The prisoners stayed in Chunggang for only a week before leaving on November 16 for an overnight march that took them a few miles up the Yalu River to Hanjang-ni where they would remain until March 29, 1951. Although their harrowing days of marching were over, the death count continued to mount during the long winter months. According to Larry Zeller, without proper clothing, shelter, and food, the prisoners simply could not overcome the debilitating effects of their days on the road. Then, too, chance continued to play a role in who survived and who did not:

The weeding out of the weaker ones that had begun the march continued at an accelcrated pace. Nor were all the ones who died among the weakest: ...*

(* Footnote: 43 Larry Zeller, 126)

And more…the same book*… Carlson's…Prisoners of a Forgotten War…page 68

(ST. MARTIN'S PRESS --NEW YORK)
(First Edition: April 2002)

(The Tiger…who was in charge of the march…referred to himself as the "Governor of the Ch'unch'on Penitentiary"...page 61 … he executed Lt Thornton on the second day of the death march).

According to Zellers, The Tiger then ordered that all dog tags be turned over to his guards to make it more difficult to identify bodies. He also forced Commissioner to sign a paper certifying that those who dropped out, including Lieutenant Thornton had died of heart failure. That done, The Tiger ordered the prisoners to resume marching…
(next paragraph)

Father Crosbie also noticed the increasingly impossible conditions of the march:

We kept on hour after hour, knowing that it would be inviting further tragedy to allow anyone to fall out…Our own plight was bad enough, but it was evident that the POWs were in a worse state. Again and again we heard the shout going up along the line: 'send back more strong men'. As with us, the weak that could still walk…

Soft Underside of Reality

It happened during the late afternoon, mandatory exercise period in the open prison yard which was surrounded by several unheated prison huts (or hutchies as the POWs used to call them). Someone threw a snow ball that hit the Sergeant of the Guard so hard and right smack in the back of his head that it knocked his hat off. This wanton act of buffoonery angered him greatly. It was to him, especially with his strong oriental upbringing, of course, a major loss of face. His rage seemed to double when he heard and realized that some of the prisoners were snickering and even laughing.

He spun around a hundred and eighty degrees and roared like a wounded lion. Wide-eyed, nostrils flaring, teeth tightly clenched, he literally ripped the walking cane from the hand of his subordinate standing next to him and charged into the group of prisoners closest to him. He swung the sturdy, oak cane violently…as hard as he could…but nothing seemed to dissipate his furious rage. Up came the cane…high above his head…down it came with all the speed he could muster, back up it went…down it came again…upon the shoulders and the heads and the forearms of those trying to protect themselves from the onslaught.

Twisting and turning he sought out any and all targets. Still venting his anger, he knowingly and recklessly inflicted as much pain as his animal instincts would allow. The men, stumbling, shoved each other, falling while raising their forearms to protect themselves from the unending and relentless onslaught. At that moment, very few, if any of the assaulted men knew anything at all about the snowball.

Finally, a merciful God made him cease the rampage. The Sergeant of the Guard stood in the midst of the fallen, broken and moaning men, six broken men in all, laying and bleeding and hurting in the fresh fallen mountain snow. He was breathing very heavy and panting like a racehorse after his race. The Sergeant's unblinking eyes bulged from his head, which swung from right to left. Despite this, he never really saw the destruction he had wrought or heard the moaning of the men laying in the mountain snow.

The guard contingency quickly formed a circle around the Sergeant of the Guard, with their bayonets fixed on their weapons, the rifle butts on their hips, the points of the bayonets between them and the prisoners. There was no need, for these men recently marched more than a hundred miles before coming to Camp Five and they were all too weak, too tired, too hungry…and yes…too cold to effectively protest.

There stood the Sergeant of the Guard, his heavy panting ebbing, with his armed guards encircling him…as if frozen in time watching the wide-eyed and fearful prisoners. When the shamed and offended Sergeant's breathing finally returned to normal, so did his military decorum.

He ordered the guards to have all the prisoners line up in ten rows and kneel in the fresh fallen mountain snow…all of them…even those that suffered his earlier wrath. They were to remain kneeling…no one was to lie down. He returned the now bloody cane to his subordinate and went to warm himself by the guard fire. After awhile, he disappeared into the hut.

The men remained kneeling until well after dark.

Now, it was very late in December and the days were much colder and noticeably shorter in the mountains and the Yalu River Valley. Since their arrival in November, the death rate did not decrease, it just kept happening. Maybe there was a shift in the causes of death. But, whatever the cause, death is seldom glorious and is always very permanent.

Clear sky...gunna be cold again tonight...I got this cough and yesterday I shit blood...my ankles, knees and wrist look double their size when I see 'em...and I don't wanna look either!!! This dull ache...constant....even my fingers...this lousy cold weather.

"Don't go on sick call….Listen Joey, your better off staying with us in the hutch…in the kooks' dispensary…dey put ya in dare…throw ya on the floor, no straw, no nuttin…an wait til ya die…ya gunna be dat much better of wid us in da hutch…ya can maybe share da blanket and da utter guys' body heat…the dispensary is shit…itz rotten!!!"

Three days earlier…

It was Joey's group's turn to replenish the water supply for the prison compound. Every five days the drum had to be filled. It was more than half a mile down a steep hill to the river…his group lost a guy last week. So, everybody gotta go and help pull the cart and bring up the water… (*Shit he can't even walk).* Down the rutted cart path, down to the river, each man stumbled along; they had to fill the water barrel. An old, lousy, rickety cart (which incidentally broke last week and had to be haphazardly repaired) was all they had to transport the huge water drum. The cart was not too difficult to handle and maneuver going down. But, the contingent of men knew that would not be the case coming back up.

On the way down, the water drum swayed slightly in the cart and it took only three guys, one on each of the cart's tongues and the other to steady the drum. Gravity was on their side going down…down to the riverside.

The return trip…the long uphill climb in the snow…slipping and stumbling…pushing and pulling and tugging…*that lousy heavy mother fuckin water barrel…*would be like looking down into the bowels of hell and seeing all your worst experiences waiting there for you.

"Steady that barrel in da middle of the cart…somebody put a rock behind the wheel…we don't want this thing to roll down on our asses…okay…dis is da way we do it…everybody gunna and gotta get wet…two guys into the river…one up to his boot tops the other up to his ankles and form a line…when we get da hand buckets…cum odda da water…and bring it to the drum…den da next two guys go in…we'll make a rotating chain…"

"Comma let's get this done…we gotta fill da barrel…comma what the fuck you doin???….you gotta get out into, ya gotta wade out a little bit…shit…whadda fuckin job…comma letz get those fuckin buckets movin…"

"…da guys from the utter groups don't form a chain…"

"Oh yeah??? Ya wanna volunteer to go in the river alone…ya dat much of a fuckin hero??? Come-on …come-on lets get this barrel filled...if you move fast you won't be as cold…"

The water started to slosh as they made their way back up the treacherous hill…up a snow covered cart path with its deep cart ruts and the occasional large hidden stones….men pushing and pulling, sometimes stumbling…and half of them believed that they would never get it up the hill. The others did not believe in anything.

Two men on the cart tongue…sometimes pulling…sometimes with their belt around a loop hole in the tongue pushing it. The two heaviest men walked backwards with their backs against the barrel with semi-squatting legs they were grunting and groaning and yes, cursing their way up the hill. The remaining two men were on the cart wheels, and like helmsmen for Captain Hornblower steering a three mast sailboat in a storm, pulling and muscling the wheel around. The large men did not alternate duties, but the others all did. When they stopped to rest, someone would make sure to secure one of the cart's wheels, to keep it from rolling back down, by putting a piece of firewood, or a rock behind it.

Another bump and a slight torque and the drum sways, slopping frigid water onto Joey and the other two guys walking backwards. "Watch where the fuck yur goin!!!...Ah dis fuckin ting weighs a ton....come-on everybody push...push...push!!!" and in an almost panic pitch... "Steady!!!...Steady!!! Steady, watch it!!! Itz fuckin sloshing again..."

Dis wedder's freezing....my feet are so cold...dare going numb...

The North Korean guard assigned to the water detail that day was one of the two that prisoners called "Karen". The sounded out "Karen" was as close as the men could get to pronouncing the guards' Korean names. So, phonetically the two became Karen One and Karen Two. Over the weeks, Karen One was christened with many other designations, other than Karen One, none too complementary.

But today's Karen...number two...was much older than the other and, as the men saw it anyway, he was not as harsh and much more understanding than his fellow guard, Karen One.

Number Two, had relatively recently been pressed into the service (less than six months ago) of the now not so glorious North Korean War Machine. Since, the Inchon invasion in September and other severe setbacks, the enemy...the round eyes...had stemmed the tide of the earlier "People's Army's Glorious Victories" in the south.

And now here he stands, in uniform, armed with a rifle and bayonet doing his part to protect their way of life by standing watch over these round eyed prisoners, from a land so far away.

Number Two had to leave a sickly wife behind with only a nine-year-old son plus a little three-year-old girl to tend to their rocky patch of not so generous soil. His older children, two sons and a daughter, have long ago left his side and were totally indoctrinated and trained ...physically and emotionally...into the surge for social justice for all classes and totally committed to the purging of the round eyes from their native land.

His sons and daughter now called each other comrade…and were taught that they were not only equal but superior to the imperialistic foreigners with round eyes. He, in spite of that brief *educational period* he was subjected to upon his indoctrination into the service, was still very confused and greatly disturbed. For he, himself, had only seen a round eyed foreigner once before in his long life, and that was at a railroad crossing with two Japanese military officers. Could these wretched and freezing round eyes he found at the prison camp really be such a threat to him and his way of life?

Look at them!!! Shivering in the cold winter air…hugging their chests…burying their hands in their armpits…stamping their feet… their noses running…staring out at you with sunken, shallow eyes…vacantly looking about…and not understanding anything…what threat is any one of them to my way of life???

Poor old Number Two had always felt he was not as enlightened as the priest in the village, or the powerful landowners, or all those men who demanded and received respect. His children too, seemed far above him in understanding the details…the meaning…of all these social injustices inflicted upon them by the foreigners.

Whenever Karen Number Two had the water detail to the river, it took much longer than when other guards were in charge. The reason was that Karen Two would allow as many breaks as the POWs needed, especially on the treacherous uphill trek to return to the camp. He never ranted and raved and yelled at the prisoners as did most of the other guards, and, in fact, even assisted sometimes by carrying and placing the piece of firewood under the cart wheel to keep it from rolling back down the hill.

Once he was reprimanded by a superior and questioned as to why it took him so long.

He replied, "Comrade Sergeant, we try to contain the amount of sloshing and water lost on the way back up the hill."

The Comrade Sergeant questioned how much could they possibly lose "…a bucket or two?" Karen replied, Comrade Sergeant this maybe true, but nonetheless the barrel is always full when we get it here and what else have the POW to do?"

The Sergeant grunted and with a quick jerk of his head stomped away. The old guard still wondered why, and could not for the life of him understand how, all these wretched and sickly men could be a threat to his way of life.

They finally stumbled into the compound, wrestled the barrel off of the cart and limped back to their hutch. They almost all immediately…or as quickly as they could…started to pull off their boots. Charlie…one of the back pushers…noticed Joey trembling and struggling to unlace his boots. His fingers were numb and aching…just flexing them...something he had great difficulty doing, became excruciating. Charlie stepped over a couple of guys and knelt by Joey to help him take off his wet, raggedy boots. Joey didn't say anything, but his eyes filled up with water.

Charlie noticed this and looked down and away quickly…more for his sake than Joey's. Charlie cleared his throat a bit and told Joe, "Just rub your feet…you'll get the circulation goin again…just keep rubbing them…"

The Cooking Fire

Gook Number Seven's hut was in between Joey's 25-man hut and another of the same size that held 29 guys. Gook Seven, as the guys called him, shared his hut with five other North Korean guards. They were armed with rifles and bayonets but Gook Seven also armed himself with a good, solid, oak cane he confiscated off an old doctor from a nearby village. He carried his weapon slung over his shoulder and preferred to use his cane and over time it served him well. His own little pain toy…he soon fancied he was as good with it as was the Sergeant of the Guard. Some of the POWs soon came to call him 'Son of the Tiger' which kind of gave him a secret little rush…Governor of the Camp!!!!

During the winter months the guards were allowed to keep their cooking fire lit all night long…it enabled them a little reprieve…a little warmth…in the bitter cold. They needed it, especially after making the rounds of all the exteriors of the prisoners' huts…most of them didn't even enter the prisoners' huts at all…because of the stench.

"What's the matter Joey?" Charlie asked.

"I'm freezing…" a pause, Charlie could hear Joey's teeth chattering, "…can't feel my feet…" a longer pause "…my boots never thawed out from the wadder detail coupla days ago…"

"Why don't you take 'em off?" Charlie didn't have to ask, for he knew that feeling of lethargy…of attempting to overcome inertia…when your body will no longer obey orders of the brain or the spirit.

"I got this stupid mom-ma-san blanket and it just ain't keeping me warm…my wrist and ankles and shoulders are aching…" another one of those frequently occurring pauses.

"Let me help ya." Charlie said.

"Naw…itz all right…I'll get warm…I'll get warm." Joey repeated, maybe more to, or for, himself than Charlie.

Charlie tried to get up, but he too was very tired and cold; he flopped back down and clinched his hands, then opened them wide and placed them between his thighs pressing his thighs together hoping for the some warmth.

There was a long silence, but if you tried hard and cocked your head slightly, you could still hear Joey's teeth chattering.

Joey broke the silence, "Charlie??? Charlie…I gotta go to the latrine," and then another of those familiar pauses, "…I need help…I can't get up and I don't wanna mess here in the hutch…"

Charlie laboriously sat up…pulled on his boots and didn't bother to lace them…he stood and helped Joey to his feet. Joey was going to tell him that he was defecating blood for the last day and half…but then didn't…*It'll stop…it'll stop soon…ya don't haf ta tell anybody…*

At the hutch door, Charlie, with Joey under-wing so to say, paused and waited for the guard to ask permission. "Hey, Number Seven, Tiger…we gotta go to the latrine…two, only two…" he used his fingers to explain. The guard, said nothing, he only pointed with his cane toward the slit trench. The POWs hobbled over. On the way to the latrine they passed the guard's cooking fire, and Joey looked at it with dull, empty eyes.

They made it to the latrine, but in reality, it was already too late for Joey. He felt the blood warming his rump and soon running down his leg. He knew then and there it would not ever stop, it was over.

"Ya ready to go back Joey…ya done?" Charlie asked in his familiar, heavy Massachusetts accent.

Joey nodded yes, and Charlie picked up his arm and draped it over his shoulder and started back to the hut. As they neared the fire, he sensed Joey shifting his weight and dropping off his shoulder…tipping and leaning toward the fire. He said, "Come-on Joey just a little bit more to the hutch…"

Charlie heard Joey say, "Naw Charlie…naw Charlie…leave me here…I can't go back…I don't wanna…leave me here by the fire…"

Joey slowly slipped off of Charlie's shoulder and out of his grasp...he sort of just drifted downward and came to rest on the snow covered Korean soil on the south side of the Yalu River. The snow had been packed and stomped down around the fire from the guards standing there to warm up after their rounds. The fire's heat radiated only so far and the cooking fire had a muddy, earthy ring encircling it within the packed snow. On his drift downward onto the packed snow, Joey cradled his head on his upper arm and when he came to rest, he smiled into the fire. "Charlie," he said quietly, "dares a pair of socks in my upper pocket...I can't get at 'em...but I want you to have em....maybe they'll keep you warm..."

"Naw!!! Naw, naw Joey...come-on you gotta get up...It is not that far...come-on..."

"Charlie...take the socks...if you don't one of the kooks will...leave me here...get out of here...Tiger Seven will be comin pretty soon...gowan...get ottda here."

From a distance, the guard...Tiger Seven...thought he saw something by the fire. As he neared the fading fire he discovered that he was right...someone was lying by the fire...*another prisoner??? Looks it...wonder if he's dead.* When he was upon Joey, he poked him with his cane and watched for a reaction. He could not tell. Tiger Seven bent deeply at his waist and tried to study the prostrate human, but remained unsure if he was dead or alive. With the tip of his cane he stirred the dying fire and, after a shower of sparks flew up, the log seemed to reignite and some yellow and orange light illuminated the body.

Tiger Seven saw the blood stain at the crouch of the trousers and from the location of the blood assumed the POW was dead. He looked around and then quickly pulled off Joey's unlaced boots and scurried to the guard hutch to store them for a future sale. The village people would pay a good price for boots, regardless of the condition.

But Joey was not dead…not yet anyway…and when the guard stirred the fire for more light and caused the shower of sparks to explode, Joey opened his eyes and peacefully watched the display. Strange…he was not cold anymore…his eyelids slowly hooded his vision of the cooking fire…and when they lifted again the sparks were gone. He looked at the log that had offered the sparks and watched it being consumed into ash.

He was breathing deeper now and recalled a ceramic pair of shapely legs on a dresser lamp…*but dat was a long time ago*...and his eye lids dropped again. They lifted and now he thought of his family at the circular wooden table in the kitchen. Strange, he was not hungry any more, probably the first time since God knows when. The eyelids again slowly dropped and remained so for a second or two longer and then laboriously lifted revealing the orange and yellow flames of the cook's fire again.

He was breathing much deeper and slower now. Last time Faustine wrote and told him they were prepping the streets for the Feast of Sts Cosmo & Damian…they were starting to string the lights over the streets from temporary blue posts. Again, the fire disappeared behind his eyelids.

And once again his eyelids lifted…revealing a dying fire…and his thoughts were of Dorie and the Blessed Miraculous Medal she sent him for his birthday. He remembered that when the guards were pulling off their dog tags, he didn't want them to have it. He thought that now his fingers seemed more flexible and he laced them together and studied the fire. His eyelids again drifted closed…hooding the vision of the dying fire…and when they once more slowly opened...that fire was now just a bed of embers. His head was resting on his shoulder near the top of his forearm, for no reason whatsoever he tried to cross himself with his free hand. *In the name of the Father, and of the Son, and the Holy*...his eyelids darkened his vision, but this time he knew they would not be lifted again…not in this world anyway.

…and…
…like Charles Dickens' character
He slept a far, far better sleep.

Burning Log

On a chilly Sunday morning in December, Tony had driven back from Utica and arrived home about three in the afternoon. As was his habit on most such return trips, he had loaded up with the 'good stuff' from East Utica. A dozen cannolis from Carmen's (*gotta save at least four for the grandkids*) and a box of assorted biscotti from the Florentine, his wife's favorite. And that was just the 'sweet stuff'.

There was sliced Italian bread from Roma's (they were enormous, two pounds apiece!) as well as two pounds of mortadella, and every other trip, hot and medium Italian sausages. Nowadays, some of the butchers put broccoli or cheeses into sausage casings along with the meat. Tony's wife and some of the kids liked it; but Tony wasn't that impressed with it. (*I don't remember that stuff when I was a kid; from what I remember the hot sausage today is like the medium/mild in the old days.*) If his wife needed or wanted something from a wholesaler...like parmesan cheese for macaroni...or some gorgonzola...the specialty houses' stuff...he'd stop on Broad Street. Tony often joked that he would almost flatten the imprint on his credit cards on such trips, but now days it is a magnetic tape that really holds the information.

Tony pondered...*we get old and obsolete in our own lifetime....Betcha Pa and Uncle Joe and Uncle Sarafino could not even accept the concept of credit cards...let alone magnetic tape...ahh...like Sinatra used to sing...dat's life!* and a little half smile raised the right side of his lips.

His Big Green (as the had named his truck) continued to charge south, down Route 8 to Interstate 88, then Interstate 81, onto the Northeast Extension of the PA Turnpike, *with all this good stuff*...and going home...going home with food…family and food…what *a nice word, HOME.*

All that was good stuff…it made him kind of happy…it reminded him of the old days. His last stop on Bleecker Street would always be at Johnnie O's bakery. Johnny was an old friend of the family, having worked for and with his brother. Johnny (like his son who is now taking over) still bet the horses and, more important, they still made what they used to call *pano Siciliano…*Sicilian bread. He'd always picked out those (at least two) loaves that were well baked…almost burned…because he liked the crispy crust, especially on days that were not humid. If…and he often forced himself not too…he put the bread in the pick-up cab, he at some point in time would inevitably take one, rip/pull it apart with his hands and devour it. God, how he loved the taste of fresh baked crusty Italian bread and ripping it apart with his hand always seemed to make him feel very masculine…very Old Country.

Pg Up

Like the kids say today…*in a heartbeat…*Tony could easily remember the entire process of making and shaping and baking pano sicialiano, as he watched his people make it in the old bakery for years. As he became older, he even helped a bit. Uncle Dan or Uncle Joe would mix the dough in that monstrous mixer and when done, would place large chunks of the dough upon the worktable. They would cover it with a large sheet so that it would rise, or as they would say, fa a repsa (let it rest). In time, it would almost double in size.

Next, they would scale the first rise…someone with a *raspa* (a dough cutter with a wooden handle) hacking at that still rising whale-sized hunk of dough, peeling away the large cover that helped retain heat as it grew. The cutter would hack a small portion of the "whale's" body…trying to get one pound, two ounce pieces. *There, that looks like it is right…*and adroitly toss it onto a vacant plate of the two plated balance scale. The other plate had two circular weights on it, one a one pound weight, the other smaller with a number two molded in the center (2 ounces), and the cutter would watch to see how quickly or how slowly the weights would rise to level position. Instantaneous decisions where made to either throw the hacked piece to one of the rollers or return it to the work table and cut some off and, then, re-weigh. Seldom, if ever, was a third weighing required.

Decades later Tony could still 'zone out' so to say, and visualize that balancing scale dusted with thousands of years of flour and those weights with the un-needed numbers and squinting at the scale to see the balancing. In time, Tony realized the trick was in how quick the newly laden plate went down...if it touched bottom it was much too heavy.

On the other side of the worktable stood the rollers, two was perfect, three too much and one would force the cutter to slow up, especially in the beginning when the dough covered so much of the table. The roller would press and knead and roll up the dough…two at a time…*ya got two hands don't ya? Use 'em…*about the size of a small cantaloupe or a big grapefruit and place them in the proofer drawers. The dough was required to rest a second time.

The men would muscle the heavy wooden proof truck (as they called them) away from the table and replace it with another. There were eight drawers in each and there were three trucks. A big batch of dough was thirteen pails of water; Tony remembered that, but not the number of sacks of flour or the bricks of yeast that were required. A thirteen pail batch required all three trucks.

The final step in the process, before the ovens, was the shaping of the bread. One by one, the trucks were again muscled and steered into position by the work table. The trucks were mounted on four very large cast iron eight-inch wheels. Every available man was used in the molding possess…both sides of the table…the more the merrier and quicker.

The one pound two ounce piece of dough came out of the proof trucks, to be pulled, punched, stretched and rolled out like a thick three foot piece of cord. Once at a comfortable length for the work, it was quickly and efficiently folded like an accordion. It was returned to the drawer, but this time it not only laid on empty (but washed) flour sacks, but was also covered with them…like a dead body. It was given another chance to rest before baking.

They stoked the fire in the ovens.

Pg Dn

When Tony got home that Sunday afternoon, he was delighted to see not only his family, but also the grandkids. It was family and food and it made Tony happy in a way that he could never relate to someone else, no matter how hard he tried.

His sons had lit the fireplace earlier in the day, and about seven, his daughter, his son-in-law and the kids left. (*Hey Dad!!! tomorrow is a school day you know!!1)*

Tony poured himself another class of Chianti, sat in the den and watched the fire. One of his sons carefully removed the screen from the fireplace, stoked the burning ember of a log, and laid two more pieces thereon. Tony watched. When he stoked the embers and the burning logs, an explosion of sparks erupted, rose, scattered and assimilated. Assimilated and disappeared. He thought of the big bang theory and he thought of the making and the shaping of bread and took another sip of wine.

Mr. Louie's Last Telegram

Pg Up

It was a beautiful September day with hardly a cloud in the sky. They used to call this type of weather Indian Summer. Mr. Louie was to retire at the end of thc third quarter of 1953. He initialed receipt of SYA603 and forccd himself to think of his forthcoming retirement. To think of his baby granddaughter and the good times coming. IIe called the messenger boy and gave him the assignment. "Do you know this address? It is by Brandcgce School" Yes the boy knew it... "Okay, deliver this."

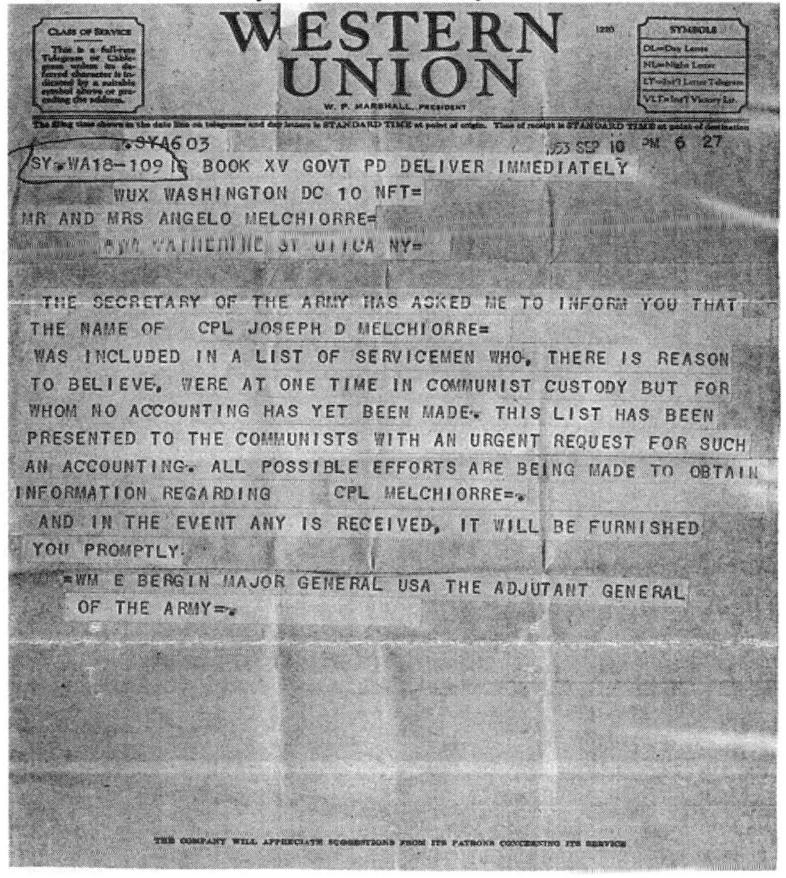

WESTERN UNION

W. P. MARSHALL, PRESIDENT

SYA603 1953 SEP 10 PM 6 27

SY.WA18-109 IG BOOK XV GOVT PD DELIVER IMMEDIATELY

WUX WASHINGTON DC 10 NFT=

MR AND MRS ANGELO MELCHIORRE=

[illegible] ST UTICA NY=

THE SECRETARY OF THE ARMY HAS ASKED ME TO INFORM YOU THAT THE NAME OF CPL JOSEPH D MELCHIORRE= WAS INCLUDED IN A LIST OF SERVICEMEN WHO, THERE IS REASON TO BELIEVE, WERE AT ONE TIME IN COMMUNIST CUSTODY BUT FOR WHOM NO ACCOUNTING HAS YET BEEN MADE. THIS LIST HAS BEEN PRESENTED TO THE COMMUNISTS WITH AN URGENT REQUEST FOR SUCH AN ACCOUNTING. ALL POSSIBLE EFFORTS ARE BEING MADE TO OBTAIN INFORMATION REGARDING CPL MELCHIORRE=. AND IN THE EVENT ANY IS RECEIVED, IT WILL BE FURNISHED YOU PROMPTLY.

=WM E BERGIN MAJOR GENERAL USA THE ADJUTANT GENERAL OF THE ARMY=.

Fifty days later: Hand written letter signed by John J Dunn.

30 oct. 1953

Dear Mr. Melchiorre:

I regret to inform you that a soldier named Melchiorre died in prison camp in Chunggang, North Korea in late December 1950 or early January 1951. I am not certain that this man was your brother but all of the facts indicate that he was. I will tell you all I know about him and you can judge for yourself. He was from Utica, N.Y. and if my memory is correct he came from a large family. I believe he told me he lived on Katherine Street. I may be mistaken because it is nearly three years since he died. I knew him very well. we had many long talks together. I particularly remember him because we lived so close together – Rome and Utica – only fifteen miles apart. we felt as though we were neighbors. If I remember right – the other prisoners called him "Sam" – was that his nickname? I am surprised that you should think that he might have decided to stay over there. you should be proud of him. He was a real soldier and a fine American and he died a martyr to the cause in the fight against communism. There were initially 738 men in our camp & 461 of them died of starvation or [illegible]. your brother died of starvation, if this man was your brother. I never knew of another man by that name therefore I believe he was your brother. If I can be of any further assistance to you please do not hesitate to ask. Please accept my deepest sympathy – Sincerely – John J Dunn

Text of John Dunn's Letter
30 October 1953

Dear Mr. Melchiorre:

I regret to inform you that a soldier named Melchiorre died in prison camp in Chung gang, North Korea in late December 1950 or early January 1951. I am not certain that this man was your brother but all of the facts indicate that he was. I will tell you all I know about him and you can judge for yourself. He was from Utica, N. Y. and if my memory is correct came from a large family. I believe he told me he lived on Katherine Street. I may be mistaken because it is nearly three years since he died. I knew him very well. We had many (begin page 2) long talks together. I particularly remember him because we lived so close together – Rome and Utica – only fifteen miles apart. We felt as though we were neighbors. If I remember right the other prisoners called him "Sam". Was that his nickname? I am surprised that you should think that he might have decided to stay over there. You should be proud of him. He was a real soldier and a fine American and he died a martyr to the cause in the fight against communism. There were initially 738 men in our camp & 461 of them died of starvation or were shot. Your brother died of starvation, if this man was your brother. I never knew another man by that name. Therefore, I believe he was your brother. If I can be of any further assistance to you please do not hesitate to ask. Please accept my deepest sympathy.

Sincerely,
John J. Dunn

Soft underside of reality

Faustine sent her younger sister Angela to Dorie's house to ask if she would please come over to their house for a few minutes. Dorie wasn't home yet, she had just started a new job downtown at Woolworth's her mother told Angela this, and quickly reassured her that she'd tell her as soon as she got home. "It'll be about five thirty."

Contribute it to woman's intuition or motherly instinct, but Dorie's mom, who had only one son, but five daughters sensed something was awry. When Angela left, Dorie's mom took off her apron, changed into one of her Sunday dresses, and went to the bus stop to wait for Dorie to come home. She assigned one of her older daughters, Phyllis, to set the table and feed the family when Dad (and not Pa…because they were more American) came home. They were going to go together to the Melchiorre house because a mother of six just knew when something bad was afoot; she would support her daughter and anyone else who needed support.

As mother and daughter walked from the bus stop on Bleecker Street to the Melchiorre house, Julia (the mother) told Dorie where and why they were going. Her gray, apprehensive thoughts and worries got darker. She knew…she just knew...something bad was happening.

They named this sweet child Dorie, Delores, after one of her husband's favorite aunts. Julia knew that Delores meant pain and sorrow and she secretly hoped that it would not apply to her little sweet Dorie…who was always so good to everyone.

She vaguely remembered her husband's Aunt Maria Delorrata and recalled her to be happy and content with so very little. No matter what happens at the Melchiorre house in a few minutes…*Please God!!! Please God...don't hurt my little sweet Dorie...please...I beg you...Hail Mary full of grace, the Lord is with thee, blessed are...*

Mother and daughter went to the Melchiorre's five-room flat, sat in their kitchen and received the news. The women sat at the kitchen table that had a platter of homemade cookies on it and an espresso coffee pot with demitasse cups and saucers and little spoons. (In the neighborhood they used to call those coffee pots machanettas*...little motors...and the kids wondered why.)*

At one time or another and sometime in unison, they...the women in Joey's life...all wept.

Tis of Thee…My Home…Sweet Home

Are The Kids Coming Over?

Pg Dn

It was one of those beautiful fall mornings…comfortably cool…big puffy white clouds in a light sky-blue backdrop. It had been an exceptionally hot summer, which had required constant watering for those plants Tony so diligently planted in the spring. Tony was secretly happy with the knowledge that now it seemed he would no longer have to unroll and drag the green garden hose off of the spool and walk it down to the lower garden, then go back to turn on the water. He'd no longer muscle and tug and loop and step over and around that hose directing the two foot long metal garden extension wand that had a beautiful big sprinkler on its end. It was perfect for watering the plants directly.

The garden hose could have been a very long light green snake, which had for its head, a yellow metal attachment that ended in a three inch round sprinkler head. Water would rush out of it and softly spread out the droplets and fall on the thirsty earth at the root base and upon the leaves of the various plants. The foliage would nod their thanks. This snake did not emit venom, but water…just gentle God sent water…half of the ingredients for sustaining life, the other half bread.

Ya want to water da plants and get da water to dare roots...not da weeds...we're waterin the veggies and not raising grass clippings.

No secret, Tony was getting older and what was years ago a pleasure, now had becoming a troublesome chore. And there was the fig tree that needed water too, and the narrow but long 'wing gardens' (as he called them) on both sides of the house and then the re-rolling of that long light green snake with its yellow wand and sprinkler at its head. Ugh!!!

Sure!!!...He knew he did not have to do it…gardening, but…but…there was something else that drove and possessed him to do it. Neither of his brothers took to gardening as he did…and Tony's mother would often tell people…*he isa moore likea his fadder dana da udder boys*…but Tony felt he had to and…in his mind…no explanations, excuses, or even a reason were necessary…*Case closed…I wanna and I'm gunna do it!!*

Like the grumpy old man that you've really become and are...sometimes...not all the time...just sometimes...you feel you gotta have your way...and sometimes...just sometimes. You know nobody really gives a damn about what you want...and life goes on. Tony smirked at his new found philosophic wisdom and a mental vision crossed his brain of a recent doctor's visit where he himself opened the discussion of the 'aging process' both physical and mental.

You must remember...you're a has been and never was...it is not what you want dat makes you happy...it is what you do with what you got!!! Dats it…Case Closed!

On this beautiful fall morning he sat at his kitchen table and peacefully looked at the garden window over the sink and felt very content to see a small basket overloaded with ripening tomatoes and a couple of garlic clusters, plus other tomatoes randomly scattered on the window sill. Those props, plus the various indoor plants he and his wife liked to maintain and displayed upon the glass shelf above, which also was 'home' for little knickknacks of small pottery. There, on that almost too cluttered shelf, was a small beige, four inch tall plastic statue of St. Anthony…right there…smack in the middle…made a picture Tony thought was worthy of a front cover of *Better Homes and Gardens* magazine.

He loved his house; his backyard with the bird bath, the arbor, the fig trees, the veggie gardens, the huge maple, the two oaks (one of which is a red oak…he planted for his first two grand daughters). He loved the inside of his house; his Italian marble vestibule, his furniture…his Persian rugs, his hardwood floors in the living and dinning rooms, his gray tiled den and his remodeled kitchen. He loved all of it, all of the upstairs and…Never…never once…did he forget the cold-water five room flat…second floor rear of his youth…of the days of Catherine Street.

And yes…yes indeed, Tony would gladly turn over his gardens and plant his garlic and wrap his fig trees and in the spring would plant veggies, disembalm his fig trees, reap his garlic and pull and muscle that long green snake with a yellow metal attachment with its gentle sprinkler head and give water…life… to his plants and labor. Yes he would…indeed he would should God give him the health and strength to do so…because as he would tell you…*this is mine!!!* He remembered with a deep sigh of resignation, the sea gulls circling and screaming and trying to protect what is 'theirs' over the municipal dump in Belize. But I am not an animal.

Sure!!!...Sure he knew that he could never had done all this alone, and sure he knew that some…maybe more than half…of his peers…have more and have done much better…but what he was looking at was HIS and his wife's and his children's. He owed it to his wife and to his parents who chose to come to America and make untold sacrifices for the benefit of the family. What if he and his brothers were born in the Old Country? Would he have fared as well? Secretly, he thought not. His mother and his aunts always describe the life there as an on going hardship…his father not as dramatic…would always say you have to work hard anywhere you are and he would play the Italian lotto every Sunday morning after Mass. The lottery tickets came printed on colored paper…not rigid or flimsy but cheap and they were orange or green or a faded yellow and they would show the previous week's results by the abbreviations of Italian cities…RA, NA, MI, FR (Rome, Naples, Milan, and Florence) etc. His father dreamed too.

Tony's father would study and analyze the results on Sunday mornings after Mass in comarra Louisa's smoke and newspaper store; they're on the 700 block of Bleecker Street. Over Sunday's diner of macaroni in a thick rich tomato sauce and a bowl of meats…some sausage, some meatballs, some spare ribs, etc. he would tell his wife and his sons, "When I win (never ever if I win) we will buy and roast a sheep and we will call all our friends over and have a feast!"

Tony not only thought…but also sincerely truly believed his talents were limited…and he only got as far as he did via moxie and a lotta, lotta, lotta luck. His dreams were like his father's…and yet…maybe not…Tony's father never met any of Tony's children and only the first two of his eldest son's children. The two little girls brought him great joy, although neither of them have any memories of him today.

Now Tony sits in his beloved kitchen, in his beloved house, and can see a portion of his beloved back yard and because he knows he, and he alone, has been the luckiest of all, muses on his good fortune and gives nominal attention to the unknown.

In this idyllic paradise, plans have been made to have their youngest granddaughter as a solo house guest for the weekend. Ahh!!! But the *best made (laid?) plans of mice and men* are for naught, and a change…a postponement…has to be made. It disappointed the 'sense' and the 'want' of being a grandfather with her little hand in his for a whole week-end. There will be other times.

Pg Up

When offered, Tony eagerly accepted the new position he sought, even though it meant leaving Utica and relocating some miles away. *Hey!!! The future is ahead of us…work hard…do a good job…you can come back as a regional sales manager…you got the world by the…in five, ten years come back home like those conquering Roman Generals.* He believed it and his wife did too.

In those early years that followed the relocation things changed and stayed the same. There was, and will continue to always be a death, a birth, a wedding, a holiday, a joy, a profound disappointment, and so it went. Tony and his wife and kids would make numerous trips 'home' during the first couple of decades and somehow or other, Tony never stop calling Utica 'home'. Even after Ma died, he still called it home, to him the words Utica and home were synonymous. He sort of shared the word home with Utica, but he did not, in his way of thinking, share the word home with his Pennsylvania address.

Uncle Dan was the first to pass away shortly after the transfer. He was Tony's favorite Uncle and when Tony lost his father so many years ago…when he was mentally more than physically immature (just leaving his teens) it was Uncle Dan that he secretly chose to fill in that void and, in a left-handed kind of way, as he ripened and matured, he made him the benefactor many little acts of kindness. Publicly and privately he tried very hard to be respectful and understanding. He never again argued, nor thought himself superior to the old man who smoked Tuscany cigars. Tony indeed had his hang-ups about how he often times thought himself superior to his own father. The lack of proper respect for him would haunt Tony forever more. Various repenting means were practiced and abandoned in his efforts to atone.

The kids were in elementary school and the viewing/wake was a weekday. Tony went up alone and stayed at Ma's flat, where she still lived on Catherine. It was only a one day viewing, afternoon and evening hours at Carmen Ennance's funeral parlor and Tony's older brother Sal, and Johnny Dee and his brother DeeBee, met afterwards at Ventura's for a couple of beers. They talked of kings and fools and a very special uncle who came to America and would not be pushed around.

....And as they continued talking about the old times and sipping their beers...Tony remembered something but deliberately refused to put it on the table for discussion...knew he wasn't going to do that...he remembered crystal clear the day Uncle Dan's eldest grandson returned from Vietnam...and Donnetta was beside herself with joy and excitement and...of course...relief...Tony was one the first she called, "Yes! Yes!!! He's home...He is HOME...no...here in Utica...he is Home. Ant-knee and his father have gone to pick him up at the airport...no...no. He didn't tell us nothing...we thought he was still out there in California getting ready to go to North Carolina he wanted surprise us..."

Tony cleared work with his supervisor, called home, picked up two bottles...one Wild Turkey...the other Jack Daniels and drove to Donnetta's house...the gray two-family frame house Uncle Dan and Aunt Grace bought in 1954. After he parked on the Jefferson Street side and was walking up to the house, he quickly scanned the first floor row of windows...the first two on the left being the kitchen windows...he saw some activity...gripping the necks of the two bottles in their brown paper bags he quickly stepped up the rear porch into the twisting hallway and burst into the crowded kitchen. And there was young Danny standing between the fridge and the kitchen sink dressed in his heavy winter wools...sans hat and tunic...his necktie loosened but not undone. As soon as they made eye contact they both shouted, "HEY" and hugged one another. Tony can still hear the little cling when the two bottles touched as he crossed his forearms around the young Marine's neck...and as the afternoon wore on...the bottles would eventually be referred to as *mustering-out liquids* and thoroughly drained.

Dan's younger brother Ant-knee went to get Tony's mom and the grandparents at the bakery. Aunt Grace woke up her husband and when he was ready…the women took off their aprons, locked the bakery door, and went off to see Danny. Strange, and yet not so strange, when the grandparents (and the great aunt) struggled up those four steps in the hallway and arrived at the kitchen door…the room became silent…Donnetta with her lips tightly pressed together and tears flowing down her cheek was consumed with pride and happiness…a clear path seemed to miraculously open allowing them to walk directly to Danny.

Aunt Grace first…she wept openly and chanted "Grazia a Dio…Grazia a Dio." Dan had to stoop over to receive her kiss and in turn he kissed her tear soaked cheek. Dan straightened up and then came his long widowed great aunt and he stooped again feeling thickness in his throat and acceleration in his blinking rate. "Ama glad…ama glad you all right," she said as they exchanged kisses. Tony's mom stepped away and then there was Uncle Dan, the grandfather, looking directly into the eyes of his first grandson…and the 'boy' looked straight back into his grandfather's eyes. Tony captured all this scene in a fleeting second and he had to turn away…neither man had to stoop to embrace…Tony distinctly heard a deep gasp and a half of a sob…and he knew…he just knew… it did not emit from the grandson.

Naw!!! Dares no way in hell…that Tony would share that with anybody…and certainly not on the eve of his eternal rest.

He wanted everyone, himself included, to remember Uncle Dan as the giant of a man who came to America and would not be pushed around.

A Nonna and a Nonno

Grandparents…
Chromosome contributor …twice removed…
Twenty-three…divided by two…and then, again
divided by two

Tony, his brothers and all of his cousins never knew any of their grandparents. Uncle Dan could not ever be what Tony would consider a substitute grandfather for him, even while his own father was still alive, he could not place him in that make-believe hierarchy. The person who filled the position of grandfather in Tony's little world, and truth be known that of his brothers and all of his cousins, was Uncle Joe.

Uncle Joe was a natural, he was the first to come to America at age twenty… 1905…the year Tony's mother was born. His young sibling that followed him across the ocean became his charge and in 1913 when his father reached Ellis Island but was turned away…the die was struck and to all the nieces and nephews born in America Uncle Joe was the patriarch. Even Tony's mom and her sisters would refer to him as Zio Joes, (Americanizing him by calling him Joe and at the same time making his name plural for some reason or other). Uncle Joe and his wife…also a Grace…worked hard and saved and dabbled a bit in offering mortgages and had no children of their own.

Uncle Joe did learn how to sign his name but never really knew how to read or write. His father abducted his mother at age 14 and the scandalous incident had forced a marriage in the practiced customs of the Old Country. He was born in a very humble household, which grew into a family of eight (with two miscarriages). As the eldest son of a transient farm laborer, Uncle Joe had to find work and did so at the village's granary. He walked a donkey in circles to crush grain into course flour. Then he would rest the donkey while he would scoop up the flour and carefully place it into a nearby wooden barrel. He would then shake out another sack of grain onto the stone wheel track of the granary. The donkey rested. Then taking hold of the mule's harness bit near the animal's ear, he'd give it a little jerk, cluck loudly, and start the process all over again.

He would never forget that he had worked harder than a donkey…and longer.

He eventually found employment in a bakery and for all intent and purpose, never left the trade. Economic conditions…*la miseria e' lo bisogno* (misery and need) left little time for the education of a young boy…especially the eldest with two younger sisters.

Nonetheless, at age sixty he sold his bakery to Tony's father and Uncle Dan, (ten year mortgage) and both he and his wife retired with a modest savings account in the now FDIC insured bank on Bleecker Street. None of the kids saw it…and probably none of the adults either…but the kids all heard and believed…he and Zia Grazia left the bakery on Pelletterri Avenue with two (maybe three) shoeboxes filled with cash. Maybe Uncle Joe couldn't read, but he could certainly count.

Shortly after the sale of the bakery, Uncle Joe and Aunt Grace moved out of the old neighborhood. They were the first to do so. He had purchased what to Tony and the rest of the kids was the biggest and the best house on Blandina Street, on the other side and way above Bleecker near Mary Street School. It was a palace…a great big white palace…two stories with a cellar and an attic…and just one family! Donnetta and most of the other kids called it a 'bungalow' because it was one family, but one of the kids heard in Miss Bailey's class that a bungalow is single story and has no basement. The class was studying about India at the time.

"So who cares what your peak nose teacher Miss Bailey sez???... It's still just only one family and it's as big as a palace and its gotta three foot high iron fence round it with an all brick fence post and a car garage fur two cars and concrete paths right up to the garage doors for the car tires. It's a million times better than a bungalow anyhow!!!...And Uncle Joe isn't got any cars and he doesn't drive nedder!!!"

Tony now smokes Tuscany cigars himself (originally cigarettes) and drinks his red wine just like the men of...and...in his youth. His thoughts of yesterday's wonderments float in and out of his waking and idle thoughts. It was alright for Uncle Joe back in those early days, but times changed and in his race with progress there was no question about the end. Time, his wife's illness, some questionable purchases all combined to sap his shoe boxes...regardless of the actual numbers...and he passed on a once rich man...who at the end would buy his Tuscany cigars, not by a box of fifty but singly, two each day.

Pg Dn

Tony got up out of his kitchen 'Captain's Chair' (as the kids call it) to again look out of it into his back yard. The arbor, the fig trees, the bird bath, the enclosed patio, the fountain with its Cherubs, the huge maple, the granddaughter's oak trees, all of it!!! Mine...Mine and my family's...ours...maybe it is not as much as most...and maybe a little bit more than some...but it is ours...my wife's and the kids' with the equally divided chromosomes.

"Did ya talk to your daughter on da phone today?" and without waiting he continued, "When are we gunna see da kids again?"

At times, and probably much more than often, such dictatorial *lines* of questioning and certainly his anguished tone annoyed Tony's wife. Nonetheless, with a patience she had been honing for years, she replied calmly and in pleasant manner, "Oh Tony!!! You know how busy she is…with the kids…No…she didn't call and I am not going to call her interrupting what she is doing…or trying to do...just because YOU got nothing to do and want some company…she'll call when she's got time or when she needs us…why don't you go rake some leaves or something or go down in the basement and do something!!!"

He half smiled at the reprimand and grumbled, "Naw I don't wanna do any work now." He recalled the lyrics to an old Jim Chapman song 'Cat's in the Cradle' *...don't know when dad...but we'll have a good time then.* Still at the kitchen window Tony refocused from the yard to the display on the garden window's shelf and sill. The tomatoes ripening in the gathering basket, the garlic flaking off its paper thin skin, and looking at the shelf and seeing the plants and the small plastic statue of St Anthony holding a two or three year old baby Jesus. *What did Ma tell ya? St Ant-knee of Padua prayed so hard...baby Jesus came to his arms. Yo!!! That's got to be better than a cat in a cradle! Never liked cats...can't seem to trust them. Sneaky little shits...and some people pick'em up an kiss 'em!!!*

God he loved this home…this domain…such a long way from Catherine Street…but only in distance. Then a phrase he had heard all his life took on a new and closer meaning to him…*Of course!!!* ***This*** *is the American Dream!!! Yur braggin! Yur braggin! Itza sin!!!*

If pride is a venial sin, then shame must be a mortal sin because shame always destroys the spirit.

Pg Up

Tony was going to get married that year, in October, and in the early part of the year he purchased a small home with a very large lot. Secretly…because he would never openly admit it to anyone…he was so proud of himself for being the very first of his generation not just to buy a house (others, including his brother Sal had purchased houses) but none purchased a one family...like Uncle Joe did in 1943. It needed work, but really not that much and he had enough time (with a little help) to shape it up.

In mid-June of that same year, the Sunday right after the Feast of St. Anthony, Tony picked up Uncle Joe and Uncle Dan, at Uncle Dan's apartment over the bakery. The pick up was pre-arranged. It was already twenty years since Uncle Joe moved out of that apartment and Uncle Dan and Aunt Grace moved in. Uncle Joe's Aunt Grace had passed away almost two years ago and time was starting to hang heavy on Uncle Joe's hands. Hands that never have gotten used to his long retirement and which in a sense compelled more numerous visits to his old haunts, especially the bakery.

He would visit his sisters at the bakery at least twice or three times a week, to get his 'daily bread': an oral agreement stated and willingly accepted at the time he sold the bakery. *Io non paga.per il pano fine che io mora.* (I will not pay for my bread for the rest of my life). It need not have been said aloud or agreed upon, his sister would have let him share and eat the bread anyway.

The house that Tony bought was in the suburbs...New Hartford...and on the ride over Uncle Joe and Uncle Dan reminded Tony that when they came to America, all this or that terrain (terreno) was isolated farms and woods (*bosco).* When they arrived, Tony quickly got out of his automobile, opened both doors on the right side and helped Uncle Joe a bit getting out. Uncle Dan was able to manage on his own and with some effort climbed out of the back seat. He had a brown paper bag in his hand.

All three of them toured the white ranch house with dark blue shutters and an attached garage. The seniors agreed there was ample room to start a family and if needed lots of terrain to put on additions. Tony did not take them out in the back yard because the property sloped away at a pitch he knew would be difficult, especially for Uncle Joe. There were two chairs in the small kitchen and two workhorses supporting an old door. Uncle Dan with an open palm put his hand to one of chairs and said to Uncle Joe, "A sede" (sit).

He did so, turned slightly to the left, looked out the single kitchen window into the sprawling back yard, and through his thick cataract adjusted glass lenses, noticed the two huge weeping willows that cornered the back yard property line. He said, "Aye!!! Le ableri che piange…bella!!!" Until that day, Tony had never heard the name of the tree, weeping willow, said in Italian.

Then Uncle Dan took out the bottle of grappa from the brown paper bag he brought along from home and had toted throughout the tour. As soon as Tony saw the bottle, he realized and quickly apologized that he had no glasses. Uncle Dan smirked and said, "Whatza da madder? You gotta a dee-zza or some ting?" With that, he unscrewed the cap and handed the bottle to Uncle Joe.

Uncle Joe took the bottle, made a quick wrist adjustment as to enable him to see the color more than the label, the color being clear, he asked, "Grappa?" Uncle Dan nodded and then Uncle Joe turned to Tony and said, "Bravo! E' Buon fortuna!" (Good for you and good luck.)

The men passed the bottle around a couple of times, smoked and talked of kings and fools. Uncle Dan gave the half filled bottle to Tony and wished that his house would have some bread and food within its walls.

A couple of week's later Tony's Ma came home from the bakery and had something for him. She presented it to him at dinner and said it was from Uncle Joe. It was a mostly black ten inch plastic item: an upside down umbrella, partially opened, standing between two unbuckled goulashes on a black base. The umbrella cane handle, but not the shaft was plated yellow to look like gold, as were the goulashes and just the tips of umbrella's supporting-ribs.

Ma told him Uncle Joe dropped it off earlier today and wanted Tony to accept it as a new house gift. Ma went on to explain that the item was kind of old and that Uncle Joe picked it up at a used furniture store right next to Commara Louise's tobacco and newspaper shop. She then asked, "Do you want it?" Tony didn't answer right away; he just looked away and bit his lips a little, felt his eyes watering, and finally just nodded yes.

Da old guy didn't half to do it...he didn't half to do nuttin! Tony thought as he regained his composure, and then said aloud, "Yeah Ma I want it...sure I want it!!!" What bothered Tony the most was that he knew Uncle Joe was buying his cigars one at time and no longer by the box of thirty or fifty.

Pg Dn

Almost fifty years later, there it stands, in the middle of a cluttered shelf above Tony's computer, an inexpensive plastic umbrella ornament. The clutter consists of a huge mug (chock full of pencils and ball point pens), a tankard stein with its glass bottom, (also full of pencils and ball point pens) and, believe it or not, a set of Chinese chopsticks which act as excellent storage for blue and red and green and beige rubber bands.

The umbrella ornament is not as heavily used or abused, not for nuttin...just out of respect.

He got the bottle of Chianti off of the wine rack as soon as he heard the garage door automatically closing and poured a drink. Tony was alone. The two oldest granddaughters and Grammy were off for the rest of the morning (and in all probability) half of the afternoon to do 'back to school shopping." It sincerely pleased him that the girls got along so well with their grandmother and he reminded himself of two things: one, how well his own kids got along with his own mother, and secondly, he himself, because it could be personal, did not feel any rivalry for the kids' attention when it came to sharing with Grammy. He truly wanted both…kids and his wife...to enjoy each other's company, and they indeed did so, especially when spending money. *Must be in the genes of women...this stuff about spending money...touching everything in the store and calling it shopping.*

What the hell!!! It is only money!!! Clutching the neck of the wine bottle and carrying the half-full wine glass, Tony elbowed open the patio's sliding door and went directly to his 'throne' (the brownish plastic chair that is guaranteed to support 300 pounds). He plopped into it, it held; and he knew it would…*you're a fat ass but you aren't any three hundred yet!!!* Tony checked the sturdiness of the backrest by bouncing slightly, and then looked out over his kingdom.

It was all there! His shed with it's extension he designed and built, the tremendous maple tree he and his son Peter (all of seven years old at the time) carried in to the yard and planted, the white bird bath currently loaded with leaves and murky water, the much smaller but prolific pear tree, planted the same day as the maple tree by his other son Raymond (all of 5 years old at the time) and Tony's father-in-law (Raymond L), the enclosed outside 'miniature courtyard' with its white painted cedar fence forming half an enclosure, four herb gardens, two very Roman looking benches and that magnificent fountain with two spouts, large concrete squares flooring the non-herb producing area.

Che va cercera? (What more do you want-what more do you seek?)

He took a sip from the wine glass, slowly swallowed, but kept the rim of the glass resting on his lower lip. Over the portion of the rim that was near his nose, Tony surveyed his lower lot. It was all there!!! His eyes darted over the rim, the arbor, the statue of St. Francis of Assisi, the cluster of figs trees (soon to be enclosed for the winter) his shrinking veggie garden, his rich loom enclosure, and it was all there!!!

Again he heard…*che cosa cercera*? (What more do you ask-what more do you seek?)

He put the glass down on the patio table, found and lit up the last Tuscany cigar he had in the green, red and white box and watched the blue smoke rise and dissipate in the cool autumn air.

The autumn of his life.

The voices that he heard asking 'what' were from the many ghosts of his past. They were the voices of people he knew…he just knew…loved him unconditionally and sincerely…without wax…like pure white marble. And they would be his father, his mother, Uncle Joe, Uncle Dan and Uncle Dan's beloved Aunt Grace.

Pg Up

On that Saturday morning, when Tony, tense but in control, brought his wife to the hospital to give birth to their first child, Uncle Joe happened to be a patient in the same hospital. He was on the fifth floor and maternity was on the third floor. During the course of that long all-day delivery…first-born births always seemed so long and 'laborious'…(must be the learning process)…and the second is like a trip back home after a long ride…(appearing to be somehow much shorter). Tony would occasionally step out of the maternity prep room and go into the waiting room lounge by the elevators.

Just like they did in the old time movies when expectant fathers would chain smoke cigarettes and pace the floor, Tony played the part. On one such 'break', in order to avoid the supervising head nurse's strategically laid-out out post, her desk was right there in front of you as elevator doors automatically glided open, he climbed the two flights of stairs. "Do you have a pass?" "No? Visiting hours are, as posted down in the main lobby, from 1:30 to 3:30 in the afternoons and 6:45 to 8:00 evenings. No exceptions and only two to a room…you'll have to go to the main lobby, and wait there. Be sure to get a pass with the room number."

Tony knew of the drill more from word of mouth than anything else. He knew too, that the rules were strictly enforced, which only served to have him apply the old street adage, *the first rule is that there is an exception to the rule.* Fortunately, the head nurse was pre-occupied giving instructions to a few candy stripers and her head was turned. Tony ran the gauntlet and soon found Uncle Joe's semi-private room. The other patient required oxygen in the room and no smoking signs were prevalent.

Uncle Joe was glad to see Tony…and Tony explained why he was there…and Uncle Joe was pleased for the second time. He dutifully inquired how his Uncle was and they exchanged niceties. Uncle Joe had been in the hospital for 4 days now, and most of his visitors came in the evening. Tony told him, that tomorrow Sunday, he was going to bring his mother and Zia Grazia to see him.

"Per vedere a mei…o la bambina che vengo?" (To see me, or the new baby that's coming?)

Tony chuckled out loud, raised both hands above his shoulders level, spread his fingers wide and said, "A tutta a due!" (The two of you!)

Uncle Joe had some Tuscany cigars in his bedside dresser. He told Tony he had not smoked in two days. With Tony at his side they slow walked to the sun porch-lounge area of the floor. They sat by an opened window. Tony lit up a wooden match and offered the first flame to the old man. He kept the flame slightly below the cigar tip and watched his uncle roll the cigar with his fingertips. Then, he lit up his cigar, whipped his wrist and tossed the matchstick in a nearby ashtray. Tony thought to himself…*Dats da way you light up dese cigars...you must use a wooden match!*

The Saturday afternoon visit lasted almost an hour before he returned again to the third floor. His wife was in the early stages of childbirth, and her discomfort was increasing with the more frequent contractions, it made him wheeze, Tony never like seeing loved ones in pain, he would wish it could be transferred to him.

His first child was born at 22:35 hours according to the hospital records, and he saw him a little bit after eleven, all bundled and capped with a pink little round face with tightly shut eyelids. It was late, but he called his in-laws from the hospital and he remembered that he had to ask the night nurse for change for a quarter.

He emerged into the hospital parking a bona fide father. He wanted to have a drink and tell the entire world of his great accomplishment. By a quarter to twelve, he was standing at the bar in Rufie's offering and receiving drinks to celebrate the occasion. At closing time, he did not go to his home in New Hartford, but instead to his mother's flat on Catherine Street.

Ma was in bed, but far from sleeping and remained in bed as she patiently listened to her inebriated son reliving the important events of that day. With the understanding and knowledge and love of a long widowed mother she told him. "Dats a good. Tony dats good…Go to bed now…we talk in the morning!"

"Okay Ma. We will talk in the morning."

He went to his old room, undressed and got into his old bed, which was never new to the family since it was purchased used. Ma and Pa would pride themselves, however, that the mattress and the bedsprings were new.

With the help of the celebratory liquid, Tony soon drifted off to sleep.

His last waking thought of the long day was of a bundled up baby in a hospital nursery and lighting up a cigar for his Uncle. On that magical night…perhaps magical to only Tony… the eldest and the youngest of Tony's family, slept under the same roof.

Pg Up

When you think about it, Aunt Grace was a natural for filling the 'grandmother' void in Tony's life. She was Ma's oldest sister in the States, she always lived nearby…as a matter of fact, when Pa brought Ma to America they shared an apartment. Then, they hassled Uncle Dan and he had to move his family to Union City, New Jersey. However, times were as tough there as they were back home and they eventually returned. Through all that hardship and anguish and…yes, desperation…Tony's Zia Grazia remained as solid as a brick…a matriarch…only weeping at death and for the injuries suffered by others she loved. Donnetta, their daughter could have been Tony's favorite aunt instead of the sister he made her to be; the families were that close.

Pg Dn

In March of that year, between the feast days of St. Patrick and St. Joseph (the 18th to be exact) with Tony's sons long out of high school, his daughter a freshman in college, his wife gainfully employed, Tony's beloved Aunt Grace collapsed on the kitchen floor and died within the hour. As she lay on the cool linoleum covered floor, one of her final thoughts was that since she came to America every kitchen she called her own, had linoleum flooring, she also wondered why she had fallen and reminded herself mostly all…if not all…of her other rooms had linoleum. In her final conscious moments with her grandson's and Donnetta's faces floating in and out of her line of vision, she smiled broadly and remembered back in 1937 she had a circular knitted carpet for her *parlor.*

They never called it 'parlor', they called it *fronda rooma* …a crude attempt at 'front room', but that was all right, they were speaking American and were much better off than la miseria e lo bisogno found in the old country.

The kids did not come to the wake, just Tony and his wife. The family and friends got together at Donnetta's house where Aunt Grace resided since Uncle Dan died. Tony and his brothers brought some booze, even though Donnetta had ample supply. Aunt Grace would often tell those she loved that when she died, she wanted tears at the church and cemetery and a party at the house. She got her wishes.

Because it was a party, neither Tony nor his brothers would come empty handed, they drank well into the night and the early hours of the next day.

"Do you remember the time Uncle Joe was smoking his cigar at Aunt Grace's apartment over the bakery and ashes dropped off of the end…bounced off of his stomach and then kind of exploded on the linoleum floor…every body knew Aunt Grace was a clean freak and had it been anyone else…she would have ripped into him…but not old Uncle Joe…Aunt Grace looked at everyone in the room and just jerked her head…to say nothing…She didn't want to embarrass the old man any further."

"Yeah! How about the time Aunt Grace and Uncle Dan were talking at the dinner table and they said that when they were kids their eating spoons were made of wood…we were at a fancy wedding and they had zillion forks and spoons and knives by each plate…yeah…remember Aunt Grace saying *"whose gunna clean all these…whadda waste…"*

Donnetta had a good one…she started telling the story of…

Right after Pa died and before Ma moved in with us, I went to her apartment upstairs from the bakery to bring her some groceries and kind of help her start packing. The week before Father Mente gave out little plastic statues of St. Ant-knee to his favorite parishioners…one to your mother one to Ma…he gave me one too…I had forgotten about the one he gave to Ma but didn't see it laying around…I figured she may have put it in the bedroom or sumptin…anyway…I open up the fridge to put in some milk and there's St Ant-knee under the freezer compartment. I said, "Ma? Ma, whatz St. Ant-knee doin in the icebox?"

"Eha e cioccolata no???" (Hey it is chocolate isn't it?)

Everyone laughed at the surprise ending and somehow everyone felt a little bit sorry for Aunt Grace…old age and cataracts is really not something to laugh at.

Tony's wife drove him to his mother's apartment and, with the help of her mother-in-law, put him to bed. He was babbling about poor St. Anthony freezing his ass off.

The next day he and wife stopped at Donnetta's before heading home. She offered them coffee and they chatted a bit. As they were getting ready to leave, Donnetta told one or her granddaughters to *go get that thing we talked about from my dresser.* The girl disappeared and reappeared in a moment. When Tony saw it, his mouth went dry and his eyes started to get watery.

He was standing by the door when Donnetta said to him, "Here, take this, she'd want you to have it."

Her granddaughter handed him the little plastic statue. He took it.

He wanted to say thank you, but could not. He wanted to say take care…see you later…good-bye…but he could not. Donnetta sensed his anguish and asked, “Are you all right?”

All he could audibly manage to say was, “Yeah!!” He tried to say something else…but could not. He turned and left, weeping. Donnetta called out to him and he didn’t reply, soon Tony’s wife came out of the house, found him behind the steering wheel smoking a cigarette and a little more composed, “Are you ready to go?” She nodded yes, and he started the engine.

Pg Dn

Strange...this is the way it all started...whadda coincidence! On the kitchen table was the morning paper, *The Morning Call*, the political blah-blah on the left, taking up six of the eight columns, and the remaining far right double column reads:

SHENANDOAH
2 guilty in
hate-crime
beating
death

Tony read the article, “ …one sobbed as the verdict was read…” and Tony thought out loud…*So would I! Sweet Jesus...So would I!*

The Maligned Worm

Tony, in another one of his "late life" fantasy adventures, embarked on still another hair- (or is it air) brained idea. He and his grandson were going to build and maintain a worm farm. His grandson had gone fishing only three times in his young life and that was about two more times than Tony had gone but, the young boy liked it. He expressed a desire to go again, especially if his Uncles and his Grammy took him. His wife considered all this worm farm business as just nonsense, and attributed it to his advancing age, or senility, or just his love for Chianti. She wisely decided to neither dissuade him nor encourage him. Like a little puppy playing with an old slipper tossing it in the air…shaking it…resting…pouncing on it again…she'd let him go as long as he didn't*...well ...you know!!!*

And off Tony went...visualizing a sturdy, small barn by the fig tree shed to store his compost…also...an 8 ft by 8 ft plot to corral and raise the worms...paint the barn yellow like the house and his tool shed…on the barn give the roof that hip like effect...to copy the tool shed…hinge the roof on the barn for easy accessibility…so that it could easily double as compost pile...all that good stuff! He created (mostly in his mind's eye) a perfect and ideal worm farm….right by his currently enclosed (because winter was coming) fig tree house.

If yur gunna become a worm farmer...you got learn a whole lot 'bout worms...RIGHT???

He started his research and went to Amazon dot com and was somewhat surprised at what was available. *Lottaz books on dis subject!!!!* He opted for *Profitable Earth Worm Farming*, by Charlie Morgan.

Page 9 from Mr. Morgan's work:

"The two types of worms in most common use...African night crawler (Eudrdilus eugenie) and

several...lumbriciod...which are divided several species from Eisenia foetida, to...night crawler. Allolborpha (Eisenia) foetida... (is) the only proven cross in this whole phylum."

And closing the paragraph, he writes:

"...BUT THE CROSS WAS NOT ACCOMPLISHED BY MAN. NATURE, IN HER PERFECT LABORATORY, DID IT, NO ONE KNOWS HOW LONG AGO. NATURE IS ENDOWED WITH ONE ELEMENT WHICH NO OTHER EXPERIMENTER EVER HAS ENOUGH OF; TIME. ONE GENERATION OR TEN MILLION, IT IS ALL THE SAME TO NATURE."

Tony read and then reread that paragraph, and thought *WOW!!! If ya think about it...that's heavy stuff!!!* He has gone back to it several times…and it wasn't just because of the evolution of the mostly invisible worm…but something else…but what???…he wasn't sure…*nothing or everything*.

Pg Up

They were called "core requirements". One such core requirement was Biology and Tony had signed up for it as a summer course. Going to school nights and wanting to finish as soon as possible, and having heard through the grapevine an old timer was teaching the course and if you weren't serious about Biology…like not having aspirations to becoming a Doctor or Biology Teacher, this guy would cut you a break. His name was Bowman…Harry Bowman and he smoked Camel cigarettes…like Tony did.

It was an accelerated class, meaning two-hour sessions with a fifteen-minute break after the first hour.

The older guys (some…but not all, former servicemen) taking the evening course and those younger kids that smoked (which was most of them) would buddy up to each other and josh around during the break. It wasn't long before old Harry joined the all-male group.

When he did, Harry was not a college instructor or an authority figure but to any of those men under that cloud of smoke, he was…one of the boys. Many times, to Tony anyway, the subject matter of those lighted-hearted conversations and observations may have become a bit…ein bitzel… ("a little amount"…from his service time in Germany) raunchy, but were always macho. It became harder and harder to take Mr. Bowman seriously when they returned for the remainder of the class.

Pg Dn

Tony smirked and thought…*yeah…after all these years the only thing you learned and remember from that class is that a worm is a lucky fellow…he just goes through his environment and eats decaying matter and then just leaves some slime to fertilize…all this while making channels and tunnels in the earth, which…in time and when necessary distributes and funnels water…that's what old Harry Bowman learned ya!!!*

In this educational adventure into the existence of the earthworm, Tony also remembered two lines from the flick *Zorba the Greek*, with Anthony Quinn. Quinn, the Greek, was conveying to the English journalist various facts of life. One being that a woman loves a man for only one of two reasons: the first, what he has got in his head or, the second, what he has in his pants (a line Tony always remembered and chuckled over). And the other memorable line was when Zorba announces…*we are all the same…food for the worms!!!*

Dats philosophical and heavy too…when ya stop and think about it…

Tony found himself falling into that Ash Wednesday mood…*remember man you are dust and to dust you shall return.* He felt like he was slowly walking underwater…like slow motion…but understanding things he never knew…understanding everything and knowing nothing.

And the maligned worm…and we, who are so superior to this blind creature of God that devours his environment and leaves slime…we who possess and are gifted with a mortal soul…and can witness and remember a sunset and can reason logically...and touch the tips of each finger with our thumb…must struggle to seek water and food and air to survive…and chase away immigrants like diving and swooping seagulls at a landfill. We will become dust and the worm will continue to devour his environment of decaying material and leave slime, without ever killing anything…anything!!!

How old did that guy say the worm was???

How old did the newspaper say the beaten Mexican was???

When was it???…last fall…yeah of course…the Saturday before Thanksgiving…the 145th meeting of the Lehigh and Lafayette rivalry.

Tony went to the game but did not watch it; he remained in the parking lot. The stadium parking lots…Easton or Bethlehem…the scene of all the other games he and friends had happily tailgated at and enjoyed. He wisely opted to stay with 'The Big Green' this year and stand guard over the 'chuck wagon' so to say. The stadium seemed miles away for Tony, plus the climbing of stadium steps and the jostle of the crowd all contributed to a no brainer decision to stay. It was a beautiful fall day and with just the right amount of chill in the air that the warm sun, up in a cloudless sky, beautifully adjusted.

He neatly arranged two folding aluminum, collapsible and web-reinforced chairs, one to sit on, the other to raise and rest his feet, all within arms reach of the beer tub and the snack cooler. He had his own church key and used it, because now…at this stage of his life…he could dictate and afford some of his preferred wants. He liked to drink his beer in long neck bottles. And his floppy fisherman's cloth cap seemed now to only bother his wife and his daughter; but he liked that too and wore it.

He had occasion to nod and sometimes chat with people in the stadium parking lot and watched some kids further down the row frolicking…walking on their hands…doing acrobatic tricks…males and females…drinking too…having a good time. Not all are football fans who attend tailgate parties, although he himself was once one. There was, equal distance from the 'kids' party and in the opposite direction, a portable unisex toilet. It was convenient.

Just before half time, what appeared to be contracted maintenance crews drove their pickup trucks up and down the rows of parked vehicles. Tony supposed from basic necessity, and basic sanitation customs, the institutes of higher learning must have made arrangements to have the garbage picked up twice. The crews…two runners and one driver…went up and down the rows pulling out those large, blue plastic bags from the open top garbage receptacles…the size of a 55 gallon drum.

Sometimes it took both runners to lift the debris from the barrel and once out, one would drag it close to the pickup truck and the other quickly replaced the blue plastic bag. If the filled garbage bag was very heavy, both would lift it and throw it into the pickup.

Tony thought the runners…as a matter of fact, even the driver…were Mexican. They were short in stature, had ruddy complexions and straight, jet-black hair. The truck stopped not too far from Tony's happy little outdoor niche of food and liquid refreshments.

Tony lit up a Tuscany cigar, using one of the wooden matches that advertised another type of cigar, snapped his wrist and tossed the spent match onto the paved drive the vehicles came in on, but did not park on. The garbage pickup truck slowly moved up the lane toward him and stopped, momentarily, not too far from Tony. One of the runners was throwing the garbage filled blue plastic onto the truck bed, the other was inserting and replacing the new bag into the drum, and the driver was looking into the rearview door mirror, watching and ready to move.

The truck started up again, the two runners started trotting a little bit behind it. The truck glided slowly by Tony, the Mexicans all saw him sitting there, all smiled and nodded in a friendly way at an old man sitting in the sun drinking beer.

And this old man…with a funny looking fishing hat…sitting and drinking a beer…by only one of the thousand tailgate party sites…nodded back at them and smiled too. Tuscany cigar in one hand and bottle of beer in the other, he motioned with the neck of his bottle of beer to the red and white cooler and without saying a word invited them to partake. They understood immediately and laughingly declined; also without saying a word.

Tony… (that's not his real name, but…) watched them continue working down the line and then eventually turn the corner and disappear. He puffed on his cigar, watched the blue-gray smoke spread out and disappear; he always loved that too.

Huh!!! Zorba the Greek says…we are all the same…food for the worms…and me…Tony the Drunk says…we are all the same…garbage collectors.

*Sooo…*Tony thought…*it all comes down to this...dis...one of the lowest species on God's food chain…the worm…the maligned and slimy worm…the sightless crawling worm with a tiny-tiny brain…the worm who will cleanse us from our sins…the worm who will wash away our inequities…*

Tony lazily checked the remaining contents in his long neck beer bottle and turned slightly to look down the line of parked vehicles…almost half of which were pickups with their tailgates hanging down like the lower jaw of a whale. He was trying to locate the nearest trash barrel. *Not dat far away…*he then turned his head and looked into the bed of his Big Green assessing the trash that had to go…stained napkins, dirty paper plates, plastic spoons…maybe some wasted potato salad. Some of the food and condiments were salvageable, and would be taken home. *Home!!! Whadda nice word,* Tony thought.

He again looked at the big garbage drum. And it occurred to him, that if the lowly worm would cleanse the Earth…as well as himself…'it' that abides and dwells underfoot and at the bottom of the food chain…then garbage...the trash/refuse barrel must be very high on the food chain. True…trash...refuse...garbage may not live and breathe (…maybe…what is inside of an atom…another universe???) The disregarded may just be higher than homo sapiens because death and time makes everything dust.

Epilogue

Why Do They Come?

We'll call him Tony, that is not his real name but it fits the character and the story. He thought of the Mexican kid and those teenagers punching and kicking and pushing and shoving...and finally killing the poor bastard so far from home...and the thought just lingered. He sure as hell didn't want to keep thinking about it. Even the relatively new (well, what seemed new to him anyway) retired life and its routine and non-urgent chores did not totally distract him from the lingering thought. He kept going back in his mind to the savagery of man. He remembers a conversation with his mother, in the security of a place he once called home.

"Ma why did you and Pa come to America?"

"La misera. (The misery). Era forte per tutti a L'Italia (It was hard for everybody in Italy)...per tata, per nonna, per tutti (for your grandfather, your grandmother, for everyone).

Pg Up

...and like it played out in his mind...

It was perfect...the gods could not have designed it any better...a large pond...maybe a small lake...it more than doubled in volume and size in the rainy season. As the rainy season gave way to scorching summer heat, the pond...ever so slowly...daily...receded, it was like a living and breathing thing...expanding and receding.

The pond was shaped like a broken trapezoid and in the southwest corner was a cluster of trees and the pond was a little deeper. The trees provided some shade over a very limited area of the lake, which was well on its way to becoming a pond. And naturally, as the water receded the shaded area shrunk. But, even now, the shaded water still managed to remain just a degree or two cooler than that which was exposed to the treacherously hot sunlight.

Well into the dry season, an embankment would reappear around most of the circumference of the lake, a part of its seasonal journey to becoming a pond. What little life that flowed into the body of water at this time of the dry season, was from an equally rapidly shrinking creek near the northeast corner. The creek's banks became muddy and slippery…and the stream smaller by the day. It would eventually dry out and would harden and shrink as clay would. The creek bed and the lake bed would resemble a dried out brownish-orange scab covering a wound – a huge scab on the surface of the earth.

In the shade of the trees, on the very far side of the pond, a gray and mossy green log seemed to just be laying there in the water. There in the shade and the cooler water, maybe twelve to fifteen feet long, the log quietly and peacefully remained motionless. A small percentage of gnarled and weather-beaten old bark was all that could be seen above the waterline.

It was close to twilight, and at the other end of the pond a herd of wildebeest (gnu) ambled lazily along following the trickling little creek. The creek wasn't really deep enough to drink out of, so the animals sniffed the scent of water and migrated to the narrow opening, where the creek emptied into the shrinking pond.

Possibly ten at first, soon thirty, then hundreds…they all came… Why did they come? They came to drink the water. The vanguard of the herd is nudged…pushed…and shoved down the narrow creek bed and soon it is forced to fan out through the opening into the lake. Those in front find themselves now wading with water above their knees. It is easier to drink while standing in the pond.

Even though you have to surrender the natural quick agility and mobility of your body, by placing your feet in the slippery muck of the lake's floor; you have come for water. The herd members in the rear can clearly smell and some even see the water. Those in the rear push even harder and muscle their way closer, edging ever so close to their basic goal and need: water.

The herd had traveled a long way, and now it was there: there…almost at their feet. *We come for water. I gotta get some water!!! Let me in there!!! Move...I gotta have water.* And, the herd literally pushed their outside perimeter and like a balloon that is being inflated, they spread into the pond…deeper…an inch, a foot at a time…above the ankles…now at the knees. Those wildebeest already in the water appear to fight, just struggling to put their heads down into the water and drink. They are being constantly jostled and pushed forward. Still, there is pressure coming from the rear; from all those that could smell and see the water, but could still not get a drink.

That mossy green and brownish log appeared to be slowly moving…maybe just drifting…not much…an inch or two. The 'log' had four short but powerful legs that would fold in along its barrel-long torso when on land, but in the water these four limbs seemed to dangle from its body. The 'log' also had a very thick and long tail; so long that when it started to drift out from under the shade of the branches, the tip of the tail remained touching the lake floor. It literally dragged, for more that half the length of the pool, until the buoyancy of the water helped raised it and the tail became suspended in the water just like the arms and legs.

As it slowly moved there were no ripples…no wake…no sound, merely a log drifting aimless in the steamy, African twilight. When the right front and the left rear legs reached the torso they rested. In a few minutes, the left front and right rear legs slowly and easily and gently moved rearward.

The log continued to amble. The slow motion cadence of the alternating legs kept the drift as straight as an arrow. Closer…ever so close…with two eyes…two unblinking eyes, at the waterline… moving ever so much nearer the drinking and thirsty wildebeest.

We are animals…no we are not…we have a mortal soul…you can live a little while without food…but you cannot live without water…everybody dies… those who are not born do not die…but without water…without water…I have instincts…like an animal…and a brain…like an animal…I can learn by rote…like an animal can…but there is something else…I have a soul…an immortal soul!!! Yes, Sister Mary Elizabeth an immortal soul means it never dies…it lives forever and ever…Yes Sister Mary Elizabeth it will live in heaven with God the Father and the Son and the Holy Ghost.

An older wildebeest jerked his snout out of the water and momentarily watched the drifting log. His instincts made him want to step back a little as to enable him to smell and see this floating object a little better. The press of the herd didn't allow it.

He thought, *No… just a log.*

On his right…four wildebeest down, was a young adult, he too noticed the log but his snout barely left the water, he sniffed the air, a micro-second later his snout was back in the water and his basic instincts and physical needs were being satisfied. He had not yet seen too much danger or tragedy in his young life.

The long tail of the log, which a few minutes ago was suspended in the pond was now touching the pond floor again, it had successfully traversed the deep water.

As slowly as the forearm and legs moved to propel the log across, the tail started to twist around and hook into the log's torso. The forearms and the legs were now able to touch the shallow bottom. The muscles near the hind quarter of the log tensed, the tail stiffened. Closer…those unblinking eyes…moved ever so close…to the younger wildebeest's drinking snout.

In one fluid movement, the tail sprung back like a taut wire being cut, the body of the log twisted ninety degrees, forearms and legs pushed mightily off of the lake floor, a tremendously large head and wide open jaws erupted out of the water like an explosion. Sixty percent of the crocodile's body emerged from the water on that one assault.

A column of water shot skyward, the animals near the attack panicked, but could not immediately flee. The press of the herd walled them in and they were stationery, there in the quiet pond in the steamy, African twilight. Many stumbled and fell and slipped and tried to climb over one another to flee. From the corner of his eye, the young adult, who a few seconds ago returned his snout to the water, saw the splash and the head coming out of the pond. He raised his head upward preparing to flee. His under neck was totally exposed and soon in the clutches of the jaws of the crocodile.

The crocodile completed his twisting action and, like a puppy playing with a slipper, flipped the wildebeest over on its back into the pond. It was almost totally submerged, the crocodile quickly released…and just as quickly reset his clinched jaws onto its bleeding neck. It was now dead and no longer thrashing or kicking. The log, and its prize, paddled back to the cool end of the pond.

In a few moments, the herd was back to peacefully drinking from the pond. And the crocodile…much higher on the food chain…needs protein to function…but also needs water. And with all his protein, he still could not survive without water and would someday too, just shrivel up and die.

Pg Dn

Tony read the headline again, "3 teens charged in Mexican's beating death" *(the only word in caps was Mexican....wonder why ...front page too!!!).*

Shit…it still made him feel depressed and haunted him. *Ever thing great in America...if you are white in America...I liked that musical...it was good...based on Romeo and Juliette...nothing new under the sun...*

Why is it bothering you so??? *I don't know…*Yes you do!!... *No…*yes you do!!! You don't wanna admit it??? Why??? *I'm not sure…*Think about it…go ahead think about it…Why??? *Because, I feel sorry for the Mexican and kinda of sorry for those crazy kids... they probably regret it very much…*Yes, that's true and we should...Is there something else??? *No…*are you sure…*don't make me say it…*what is it??? *No…*Come on…come on!!! *Because....because…*Come on …Come on!!! *I could have been one of those asshole kids!!! I probably was in different ways... a zillion times in my life...in my thoughts, what I have done and what I have failed to do...a million times...*Okay, once more...Why??? *Because...because…*come on spit it out…*because I am a son of immigrant!!! That makes me an immigrant.*

And dark thoughts rolled into Tony's brain…did you only want to drink??? Were you so hungry you had to kill to eat??? Did you push and shove and maneuver others to get what you needed??? It's life…it's life…Whadda ama gonna do bout it??? What??? What??

That's honest…how do you feel??? Better??? *I don't know...I just wish it was different...I just wish I was different...*maybe better??? *Yeah, better...but what the hell is better supposed to be to that Mexican kid???*

Le immigrante
(The immigrants)

Ma and Pa
Pa 'Pietro' from Cisternino, Brindisi/Bari , Italia and Ma, Chiara
nee Di Risio from Vasto, Chieti. Providence of Abruzzi Italia

Zio Giuseppe e Zia Grazia
Uncle Joe from Vasto, Chieti, Abruzzi, Italia and his wife Grace
nee Di Angleo from Vasto, Chieti, Abruzzi, Italia

Zio Sarafino e Zia Lucia
Uncle Sarafino from the mountains of Abruzzi and his wife Lucy
nee Di Risio from Vasto,Chieti, providence of Abruzzi,. Italia

Zio Donato e Zia Grazia
Uncle Dan from Vasto, Chieti, Providence of Abruzzi, Italia and his wife Grace
nee Di Risio from Vasto, Chieti, Providence of Abruzzi Italia

Angelo & Maria Melchiorre
Angelo nicked named 'Fureidere' from Arborbella, Providence of Bari/Brindisi, Italia
and his wife Maria nee Salamida from Arbrobella, Providence of Bari/Brindisi, Italia

Mikhael and Mantaha Tamer
Mike from Zahle, Lebanon and his wife Mantaha (Minnie) nee Kassouf
from Wadi el Arayesh, Lebanon

Nicolo e Anna Lo Conto
Nicolo, nicknamed Nick from Cisternino, Bari/Brindisi, Italia and his wife Annie
nee Lo Parco from Cristernino, Bari/Brindisi, Italia

&

The millions of others that passed through
Garden Castles & Ellis Island from 1880 to 1939

Le figlii delle immigrante
(The children of the immigrants)

Tony and his brothers, Salvatore & Angelo, privy to the spectral of life in the neighborhood

John Dee a first cousin everyone should have been blessed with
and who spilled blood on two hemispheres

Mr. Alito disembarked from the steamship in his mother's arms, the youngest
of seven, served in France WW I, married Julia nee Lauria and raised a family

Donnetta & Faustine from different households…both ***Big Sisters***
in every sense and meaning of the words

Mike one of Mikhael & Minnie three sons…a sailor who once went far
away to sea and learn how much he loved his home

Joey one of thirteen whose fate and

final outcome matches the unfortunate number

Frank LoConto the ball player with athletic motor skills that Tony
envied and Paulie could only dream of

Le amici e amici de amici
(The friends and the friends of friends)

Hatbox Becky a painted woman….with baggage… who like so many of us
often wished and dreamed she was someone else

Mr. Louie a sensitive and caring man whose eyes would fill with tears whenever
he heard the finale of The 1812 Overture…always listening for the church bells

Johnny the Hammer…only a half man in physical stature but a
fierce and raging giant when called to protect

La Fransica a beautiful understanding woman who deserved something
A lot better in her short life

Anche
(also)

A boy on a bike with an oversized hat